INTRODUCTION:
IMPORTANT FACTS

My name is Saxby Smart, and I'm a private detective. I go to St Egbert's School, my office is in the garden shed, and this is the second book of my case files. Unlike some detectives, I don't have a sidekick, so that part I'm leaving up to you – pay attention, I'll ask questions.

SAXBY SMART
PRIVATE DETECTIVE

SAXBY SMART
PRIVATE DETECTIVE

THE FANGS OF THE DRAGON
AND OTHER CASE FILES

SIMON CHESHIRE

Piccadilly Press • London

First published in Great Britain in 2008
by Piccadilly Press Ltd,
5 Castle Road, London NW1 8PR
www.piccadillypress.co.uk

Text copyright © Simon Cheshire, 2008

A catalogue record for this book is available
from the British Library

ISBN-13: 978 185340 983 7 (trade paperback)

1 3 5 7 9 10 8 6 4 2

Mixed Sources
Product group from well-managed
forests and other controlled sources
www.fsc.org Cert no. TT-COC-002227
© 1996 Forest Stewardship Council
FSC

Printed in the UK by CPI Bookmarque, Croydon CR0 4TD
Cover design by Fielding Design

Case File Four:

The Tomb of Death

CHAPTER ONE

I'M NOT VERY GOOD AT making things. If I ever do one of those plastic construction kits (you know, fighter planes, sports cars, etc.), I always end up with it covered in patches of glue. And a piece stuck on backwards. And another piece that falls off as soon as I put the finished model on my shelf.

So I should have known better than to try to fix my Thinking Chair. As readers of Volume One of my case files will know, my Thinking Chair is a vital part of my work as a brilliant schoolboy detective. It's a battered old leather armchair, and in it I sit, and I think, and I mull over important facts about whatever case I happen to be working on.

My Thinking Chair had developed a slight rip on one

of the arms. One afternoon during the spring half-term hols, I was in the garden shed trying to patch it with a piece of super-tough heavy-duty repair tape. *Guaranteed 100% Bonding Power!* it said on the roll. The trouble was, it was one hundred per cent bonding my fingers together.

Just as I was wishing I'd asked my very practical friend 'Muddy' Whitehouse to do the job for me instead, there was a knock at the shed door. Immediately, I heard the sign fall off (the sign I keep nailing up outside, which says *Saxby Smart – Private Detective*). I sighed to myself.

'Come in!' I called.

In came Charlie Foster, a boy in my year group at school. He was an owlish kid, the sort of person who gives the impression of being tubby even when they aren't. He wore tiny round glasses, and had a habit of sniffing a lot.

He looked around the cluttered interior of the shed. Half of it, as always, was crammed with old gardening and DIY stuff of my dad's (I'd found that super-tape in amongst it). The other half of the shed was crammed with my desk, my files and my Thinking Chair.

He handed me the sign from outside. 'Hello, Saxby. Is this yours?' he said.

You can tell he wasn't the sharpest tool in the box,

can't you? He was also looking a little scared, and carrying a slightly crumpled handwritten note.

'What can I do for you, Charlie?' I asked. 'Who's told you to come and see me?'

He sniffed in amazement. 'How did you know it wasn't my idea?'

'People who need my services don't normally turn up looking as if they don't want to be here,' I said. 'Besides, that note you've got there is written in an adult's handwriting. My guess is that someone has written down some specific information.'

'Yes,' said Charlie, with another sniff. 'My big brother Ed. He's nineteen.'

'And why does your brother Ed need my help?'

'His comic's been stolen.'

My eyes narrowed. 'Hmmm. Yeeees, I can see that would be annoying. I don't want to sound rude, but, umm, wouldn't this be filed under Not All That Important? Or possibly under I'll Go And Get Another Copy?'

Charlie suddenly remembered the note, smoothed it out a little and double-checked something written on it. 'This comic is worth one hundred thousand pounds.'

CHAPTER TWO

'HOW MUCH?' I GASPED. 'What's it made of, solid gold?'

I fell back into my Thinking Chair. This made the rip in the arm worse, but right now I was more concerned to hear the details of Charlie's problem. Or rather, his brother Ed's problem. Charlie blew the dust off an old crate full of paint pots and sat down.

'Ed is a collector of comics,' said Charlie. 'He buys and sells them, and he's got shelves full of really old and valuable ones.'

'As it's a weekday afternoon, and he's sent you here rather than come himself, I deduce that he normally needs to be somewhere at this time of day. So trading comics is his hobby, not his job?' I said.

'Yes, that's right,' said Charlie, 'he works at the

8

restaurant in Frizinghall Street. He's a chef. But he's hoping to become a full-time trader. Or he was, until this comic was stolen.'

I settled down in my Thinking Chair, trying to ignore the low ripping noise that was still coming from the arm. 'So, tell me all about this comic, and what exactly has happened.'

'It's Issue 1 of *The Tomb of Death*,' said Charlie. He consulted Ed's note again. 'Published in America in 1950. There were only a few thousand copies made, and there are less than six known to still exist.'

'And what's so special about Issue 1 of *The Tomb of Death*?'

'Dunno, never read it,' shrugged Charlie. 'But comic collectors dream of owning a copy. It's one of the most valuable comics in the world, so Ed says.'

'And when was it stolen?' I asked. 'Give me every detail you can.

'Ed keeps it . . . er, kept it . . . in the wall safe downstairs at our house. Dad had the safe put in because he sometimes has a load of money in the house, if he can't get to the bank after his shop's shut. But Ed uses it mostly. *The Tomb of Death* was in a see-through plastic case, propped up at the back of the safe.'

'And how long had it been there?'

9

'Ed inherited it a couple of years ago. Our granddad used to be an avid comic reader when he was our age, and when he died he left two big boxes of old comics to Ed. And in amongst them was *The Tomb of Death*.'

'It was always kept in the safe?'

'Always. Ed hardly ever took it out. It was far too valuable and delicate to handle. It stayed in the safe twenty-four-seven!'

'Why didn't Ed sell it?'

'I think he was going to. I'm not sure, you'll have to ask him.'

'And when was it stolen?'

'Last weekend. Dad opened the safe on Monday morning, and it was gone.'

'Just like that?'

'Just like that.'

'The safe had been cracked? You'd had a burglar?'

'Ed and Dad say not. We have an alarm system, and that hadn't been tripped. The safe has its own alarm, and that wasn't tripped either.'

'Was it there on Sunday?'

'Yes. Dad put the weekend's takings from his shop in there. The comic was still in the safe then. Definitely. I saw it myself.'

'So there was a lot of money in the safe that night?'

'Yes. That's why the safe was opened on Monday morning: to get the money out so Dad could take it to the bank.'

A couple of important points had already become clear to me. One of them was about the safe, about *how* someone had gained access to that comic. The second important point was about the comic itself, about *why* the thief had stolen *that*, rather than the money that was also in there. Can you work out what I was thinking?

Point 1: If two alarms weren't tripped, and no burglar was involved, then the safe was almost certainly opened by *someone who already knew the combination* to it!

Point 2: If the thief took an old comic, but left a pile of cash untouched, then the thief was almost certainly *someone who already knew the value* of the comic. They knew that the comic was worth more than the pile of cash!

'This is all very puzzling,' I mused. 'Didn't Ed go to the police?'

'Yes, but they say there's nothing they can do. There was no break-in, or anything like that. It's as if the comic simply vanished into thin air, overnight.'

I stood up decisively. 'OK, here are the two things I'm going to do, in reverse order: Number Two, I'm going to examine the scene of the crime; Number One, I'm going to try and get this wretched super-tough heavy-duty repair tape off my fingers. Tell your brother that Saxby Smart is on the case!'

A Page From My Notebook

Question: If the comic was so valuable, why did Ed keep it? Why not sell it and get enough money to set himself up as a full-time trader, which is what Charlie says he wanted to do?

Question: What kind of thief steals a comic, but not money? Even if a thief saw a comic book in a safe and thought, Aha! I bet that's valuable, they'd surely have taken the money TOO. Why was this thief ONLY interested in the comic? I'm sure this is significant.

Question: Will I be scraping these gluey bits off my hands for the rest of time?

CHAPTER THREE

FIRST THING THE NEXT MORNING, I boarded a bus to Charlie's house. As it rumbled its way through town, I phoned my super-brainy friend and all-round research genius, Isobel 'Izzy' Moustique.

'*How much?*' she gasped.

'That's exactly what I said,' I said. 'I'm on my way to the scene of the crime right now.'

'A comic book so rare and valuable would be very hard to sell without attracting attention,' said Izzy. 'This must be a pretty stupid thief! There's no way they could *do* anything with that comic without being noticed.'

I shrugged. 'They could read it.'

'What? You're telling me that the contents of a comic like that wouldn't have been reprinted and republished in a dozen books by now? No, nobody would steal it just to see what was printed in it.'

'I guess not,' I said. 'Anyway, see what you can come up with. Information on recent sales of rare comics, that sort of thing.'

'Already on it,' said Izzy. 'Come and see me later.'

As the bus chugged and bumped along the town's main shopping streets, something struck me about what Izzy had said. She was right – the thief would find it almost impossible to sell that comic without being noticed.

Unless . . .

Unless they didn't plan to sell it at all. Suddenly, I jumped up with a cry! It startled the old lady sitting in the seat behind me.

'Have you missed your stop, luvvy?' she asked.

'No, I've missed an obvious suspect!' I replied.

She gave me a funny look. I think she thought I was a bit barmy.

But there *was* an obvious conclusion to be drawn here. What sort of person would steal that comic book and *not* intend to sell it at all? Only one sort of person, as far as I could see! Can you see it too?

Another *collector*, like Ed! Someone who might want to keep the comic just for its rarity alone.

At last the bus reached my stop. The old lady clutched her shopping and watched me nervously as I raced to get off. I hurried over to Charlie's house. He took me up to Ed's room first, so I could finally meet his brother.

They say that the clothes you wear say something about you. If that's true, then the clothes Ed wore said something rather rude. With a hand gesture added in as punctuation. He was without doubt the scruffiest person I'd ever seen in my life. He looked as if he'd bought his T-shirt and jeans from the local rubbish tip, and he had a scrubby beard that reminded me of those scatterings of sugary bits you get on cakes. Apart from all that, he was simply a larger version of Charlie.

His room, tucked away in a converted attic at the top of the house, was his exact opposite. It was amazingly neat and clean. One entire wall was covered in white shelving units, and housed on these units were hundreds – no, thousands – of plastic envelopes. Just visible inside each envelope was the outer edge of a comic book, and most of the envelopes had handwritten sticky labels attached to them.

Ed was sitting in front of his computer. As soon as Charlie and I came in, he bounded over to me and shook my hand so enthusiastically I thought my teeth would come loose.

'Hi!' he said. 'You must be Saxby. Charlie's told me all about your exploits, kid. I hope you're as good as your reputation suggests.'

'Better!' I declared with a grin. 'Now then, tell me more about this comic.'

Over a glass of fruit smoothie and some rather posh chocolate biscuits ('Ooh, yes, I'll have another one of those,' I said. 'Thanks.'), Ed told us the tale of *The Tomb of Death* with a wild gleam of eagerness in his eyes.

'Way back in the 1950s,' he said, '*The Tomb of Death* was the first in a new style of comic book in America. Full of grisly stories about murder plots, evil curses and tentacled monsters. These comics were a smash. Kids loved them. And within a couple of years, they were banned!'

'Banned?' I said. 'Were they really horrible, then?'

'Naaah,' said Ed. 'They were funny! With a few scares thrown in, mind you. The thing is, parents started saying they were a bad influence on kids, and they were all banned: *The Tomb of Death*, *The Valley of Slime*, all of them.'

'I see,' I said. 'They weren't published for long, and parents would get rid of them wherever they could.

Result: they end up as rare collector's items.'

'Precisely!' cried Ed. 'There are certain comics that are legends in the world of collecting. Like, for instance, the Action Comics issue in which Superman first appeared in the 1930s, or Batman's arrival in Detective Comics a little later. Or Issue 15 of Marvel's *Amazing Fantasy* – that's the origin of Spider-Man; that comic's worth a fortune.'

'And *The Tomb of Death* is as famous as those?'

'Weeeell,' said Ed, pulling a face and rocking his head from side to side. 'It's less sought after, but it's *so* unusual that its value is at least their equal.'

My earlier thoughts about another collector being the thief sprang to mind. 'Did you keep the comic a secret? Did other collectors know you had it?'

'Of course they knew!' cried Ed. 'I mean, what's the point of having Issue 1 of *The Tomb of Death* in your collection if you don't tell the world?'

'You weren't worried one of them might try to steal it?'

'To be honest, no,' said Ed. 'It was in that safe, locked away.'

'And it never came out of the safe?'

'Never. Well, except on special occasions, and on those occasions it never left my sight.'

'What sort of special occasions are we talking about?'

'Er, let's see,' said Ed, wrinkling his nose up in thought. '*Comics UK* magazine did an article on my collection about a year ago. They took a picture of me holding the comic. Then I took it to a trade fair shortly after that.'

'What's a trade fair?' I said.

'A kind of comic convention,' said Ed. 'Lots of traders, lots of buying and selling goes on, comic publishers show off their latest stuff, that sort of thing.'

'An ideal opportunity for a thief!'

Ed shook his head. 'That comic was in a sealed, see-through case that never left my hand. I even took it to the loo with me! It was perfectly OK.'

'Was that the last time the comic was taken out of the safe?'

'No, there was one more time, about four months ago. I took it out to show to Rippa. He's another collector. He's got a shop in town, right opposite the restaurant I work at. That's how I got to know him. Odd bloke. Not really someone you'd trust.'

'I see,' I said quietly.

Ed could see what I was thinking. 'I can see what you're thinking,' he said. 'No, he never even touched it. You shouldn't touch comic books that old, anyway.'

'Not touch them? Why?'

'They were printed on very cheap paper. High acidic content in the wood pulp, you see, so after a few years the paper literally starts to crumble. That's another reason why certain comics are so rare. Most copies have simply fallen apart. You've got to keep the air off them, and keep them out of sunlight. Like vampires.' He pointed to the neatly stacked comics on his shelves. 'Why else do you think I keep all of those in plastic wallets?'

'So this Rippa didn't even touch it?'

'Nope. I did take the comic out, and turned the pages so we could both admire the thing. Wonderful smell comes off them, you know, the smell of history. Of course, I wore cotton gloves. Even the tiny layer of sweat on your fingertips can damage that paper.'

All this time, Charlie was being oddly quiet. He kept sipping at his smoothie and staring at the rows and rows of sealed-up comics on the shelves.

'So,' I said, 'if the rest of the collection is kept in this room, rather than the safe, I assume none of these are anywhere near as valuable?'

'Correct,' said Ed, 'but there's some very interesting stuff here. Take this one, for instance . . .'

Ed Foster might have dressed like a walking rubbish dump, but he was clearly an expert on the history of comic book publishing. He showed me what made particular issues of a comic more collectable than others (Issue 33 of *The Amazing Spider-Man*, for instance, worth more than Issues 32 or 34, because it contains a very well-known story. Or, Issues 12 to 22 of *The Purple Avenger*, worth only fifty pence each because the artwork was rubbish. Fascinating stuff!). By the time Ed had given me his eager guided tour of the shelves, I was ready to rush out and start a collection of my own!

Charlie kept peeking over his brother's shoulder, trying to get a look at whatever Ed was showing me. Drips from his almost-empty glass of smoothie plopped on to the carpet.

'Oi, Charlie!' cried Ed. 'Watch it! You get any of that on these comics and you're for it! You know you're barred from the entire collection.'

'Barred?' I said.

'Yeh,' said Ed, eyeing his brother moodily. 'Ever since I let him borrow one of my 1960s *Fantastic Four*s and he got jam all over it.'

Charlie stuck his tongue out at Ed. (Actually, no, he didn't do that. Actually, he said a short sentence that included the words 'complete' and 'you', and which I can't repeat here!)

'Can I see the crime scene now?' I said quickly.

We went downstairs. The safe was recessed into the wall of the living room, and concealed behind a painting that swung back on hinges like a door. The rest of the room was just an ordinary living room: sofa, a couple of chairs, TV in the corner.

The safe had a standard combination lock, a big dial in the middle of the door that you turn back and forth to line up with a series of numbers. Ed opened it up, standing close to it so that nobody could get the combination by watching him. All that was inside the safe was a small pile of papers.

'That's all stuff of Dad's,' said Ed. 'Stuff about the house, insurance and so forth.'

'And the comic was propped up at the back there?'

'Yup.'

'In full view, so you'd know straight away it was gone?'

'Yup.'

'No way it could slip out of sight, or get mixed up with those papers?'

'Nope.'

I remembered my earlier deduction, from Chapter Two: if the safe hadn't been broken into, then the thief had to be someone who knew the combination.

I asked Ed where the combination was kept. He

tapped the side of his head. 'In here,' he said. 'There's only me, Mum and Dad who know it. None of us has got it written down. None of us has ever told anyone else what it is.'

'I don't know the combination,' said Charlie. 'They won't even tell me what it is. I've never opened that safe in my whole life.'

At that point, I had to admit I was out of ideas. The theft of the comic book seemed almost impossible. So only those three people could have opened the safe?

Suddenly, I wasn't out of ideas any more! If the thief didn't *break in* to the safe, and the thief couldn't *open* the safe (assuming, of course, that neither Ed nor his parents were the thief!), then there could be one, and only one way the thief could have struck.

Can you see how?

The thief could only have struck when the safe was *already open*.

'This Rippa bloke,' I said. 'Was he here in the room when you opened the safe to show him the comic?'

'Yes,' said Ed.

'Aha!' I cried.

Ed waved his hands about. 'Hang on, hang on! I wondered about that myself. But the comic was here when he left. Under lock and key, back in the safe. I put it back in there myself.'

'Was Rippa left alone with the comic?' I asked.

'Only for a couple of minutes,' said Ed. 'I'd just finished showing him the pages. I'd put it back in its plastic wallet, and the doorbell rang. As soon as I came back into the room, I realised what I'd done! I'd left the comic unattended! But Rippa was sitting over there, looking through some catalogues he'd got with him. The comic was untouched. Safely in its see-through wallet. He had *not* nicked it.'

I sat on the sofa. 'Hmm, yes. You'd have to be a pretty stupid and desperate thief to try to snatch that comic from right under your nose.'

'Exactly,' said Ed. 'Even if he'd *thought* about nicking it, he couldn't possibly have actually *done* it.'

'Hmm,' I said again. 'Well, someone "done it".'

I thanked Ed for the smoothie, took another biccie for the journey home ('Ooh, thanks, don't mind if I do!') and headed for the bus stop.

Once I was back in my shed, I sank into my Thinking Chair to mull over the facts. Then I stood up, pulled that wretched roll of super-tough heavy-duty repair tape off the back of my trousers, and sank into my Thinking Chair again.

A Page From My Notebook

Problem: Logic says 'You'd steal that comic in order to sell it'. BUT! Nobody could sell it without being noticed.

Problem: Logic says 'The only person who WOULDN'T steal it to sell it would be another collector'. BUT! As Ed explained, half the point of having a rare comic in your collection is to show it off. The thief would never be able to do that without arousing suspicion. (In fact, they'd have to go to some lengths to STOP anyone knowing they'd got it!)

Problem: Logic says 'EITHER the thief opened the safe, OR the thief struck when the safe was open'. BUT! Both those options now seem to be ruled out. Unless . . .

Question: COULD Ed have done it himself, for some unknown reason? OR, could his mum or dad have done it, for some equally unknown reason? Must investigate further!

Fact: Charlie is barred from looking at Ed's entire collection. Which seems a bit mean, but I suppose I can understand it. I'd bar Charlie from my shed if he started getting jam on my case files!

Fact: The rip on my Thinking Chair is getting worse. Must remember to phone Muddy.

CHAPTER FOUR

THE SIGN OVER THE SHOP SAID: *Comix Nirvana* in big bouncy lettering, with *We buy, sell, x-change* in smaller bouncy lettering underneath. Beneath the sign, on a handwritten sheet taped to the shop window was *No Time Wasters!* (I assumed this sheet meant 'serious collectors only', rather than being some sort of sci-fi warning that the shop was out of stock of something called *The Time Wasters*. But I couldn't be sure.)

The shop was tucked away at the far end of Frizinghall Street, just outside the centre of town. Opposite it, and a few dozen metres up the road, was La Pizzeria, the restaurant where Ed Foster worked as a chef.

As soon as I entered Comix Nirvana, I got the distinct feeling I was being watched. And I don't mean they had

CCTV in there. Behind the counter, perched on a high stool and flicking through a DVD catalogue, was Rippa. His beady eyes followed me as I strolled around the shop, pretending to browse, keeping an eye out for clues.

It was a small shop, no bigger than our classroom at school. Racks of action-packed front covers stretched from floor to ceiling, right around the walls. The ceiling itself was papered over with old movie posters, announcing that *IT Came From Space* and *The Astro-Zombies Have Arrived*. Beside the counter was a huge wooden box raised up on thick legs, divided up into sections. Inside each section were some of the same kind of plastic wallets that Ed used, containing comics with covers that were slightly wrinkled and faded.

'These are the old comics?' I asked innocently. 'The really collectible ones?'

Rippa nodded. He was in his early twenties, thin with gelled-back hair, and wore a creased white shirt with a loosely knotted tie. Ed had told me that his real name was Tarquin, and that anyone who called him Tarquin got something thrown at them.

'You buying?' he said.

'Yes, I might be,' I said brightly. 'My dear old gran has given me a whopping great wad of birthday money, and I thought I'd invest it in some vintage comics.'

'Wise move,' said Rippa with a smile that made me think of cold gravy. I really don't like cold gravy.

My mission at Comix Nirvana had two aims: 1) to observe Rippa in his natural habitat, and 2) to see what useful information I could gather. My investigations would meet a dead end, and fast, if I couldn't establish more facts about the suspects.

'Anything in particular you're looking for?' said Rippa. He pointed to the wooden box. 'Lots of rare items in there.'

The rackings around the walls of the shop were crammed, overflowing even, but this wooden case had plenty of space in it. I wasn't sure what this might suggest: had there been a sudden rush on vintage comics lately? Or was Rippa simply not very good at keeping old issues in stock? I leafed through the box casually.

'How about those *Purple Avengers* there?' said Rippa. 'I got the whole run from Issue 10 to 25 there. Worth fifteen pounds each, because of their age, but I can let you have them for a tenner apiece.'

'Mmm, no,' I mooched. 'I'm not really a *Purple Avenger* fan.' (This was perfectly true – for more on this, see my earlier case file, *The Mark of the Purple Homework*!)

'See that one there?' said Rippa. 'That's it, the issue of *Mars Robot Rampage*. You can take it out of the wallet and have a look. Printed in 1938, that was. Nobody's got a complete set of those, not anywhere in the world. I've only got the one issue so I'm selling it cheap, just thirty pounds.'

I took out the comic and flipped through it. Giant machines with laser guns for eyes zapped up at me from the smooth, brightly printed pages. *Destroy all Earthlings!*, *Run, Penelope – we don't stand a chance!*

That settled it. This short conversation had given me *proof* that Rippa was a crook, or at least that he was willing to rip off his customers. In fact, I now had *two* very specific proofs that Rippa was quite happy to engage in some dodgy dealing.

Thinking back to my meeting with Ed Foster, can you spot what these two proofs were?

Proof 1: Those issues of *The Purple Avenger* weren't worth anything like ten pounds each, as Ed had explained to me.

Proof 2: If that issue of *Mars Robot Rampage* really *was* printed in 1938, it ought to have been in a very delicate, crumbly state. No collector would let someone casually handle it like that! Rippa was clearly lying about its age.

'Mmm, I think I'll leave it for now,' I said.

'Don't leave it long,' said Rippa. 'You won't get offers like this from other dealers.'

'That's very true,' I said, nodding wisely.

I headed for the street. I paused with the shop door ajar. 'By the way,' I said, 'have you got the latest issue of *The Time Wasters*?'

'What?' grunted Rippa. 'No, I haven't! Can't you see the sign in the window?'

CHAPTER
FIVE

I WENT TO SEE IZZY, Queen Of All Info. Her room was looking particularly fluffy, sparkly and other girly adjectives. The chunky rings on her fingers caught the light from the glitterball attached to the ceiling.

She set her laptop to sleep and spun round in her swivel chair to face me. She consulted a stack of print-outs to re-check her facts.

'OK, two things,' she said. 'First, this Rippa character is perfectly willing to get involved in dodgy dealing.'

'Yes, I've noticed that myself,' I said. 'What did you find?'

'A couple of years ago he was caught out trying to pass a facsimile edition off as the real thing.'

'A simmy-what?' I said.

'A facsimile,' said Izzy. 'Now and again, comic companies will republish a particularly famous or popular old comic. Same insides, same covers, and so on. These facsimile editions are just casual collector's pieces, really, to give you the look and feel of what an old comic was like, without you having to actually fork out for the old comic itself.'

'That sounds a bit sneaky,' I said, wrinkling my nose.

'Oh, there's nothing dodgy about it,' said Izzy. 'These facsimiles are clearly sold as "not the real thing". They're very popular with comics readers.'

'And Rippa tried to sell one as if it was old and valuable.'

'Right,' said Izzy. 'If you know nothing about comics, it's juuust possible that someone like Rippa could fool you into thinking you were buying the real thing. Anyway, he was caught out at the last minute. He claimed it was a mistake. Which, to be fair, it might have been. But there are some dealers who still won't trade with him.'

'Hmm,' I pondered. 'Pity Ed Foster isn't one of them. Anything else on Rippa?'

'I checked the auction websites. There are several specific trading sites where comics dealers do business. One thing's for sure: Rippa has never sold, or bought, a single copy of *The Tomb of Death*. Not any issue, not ever.'

'That's definite?'

'Absolutely. And by the way, his real name is —'

'Tarquin, yes, I know. I'm trying to think of a way to see if he really does throw something at you if you call him that.'

Izzy dropped her pile of print-outs back on to her desk. 'You know, Saxby, I think you're barking up the wrong tree with Rippa. Looking at the scene of the crime, and what happened, I don't see how he could possibly have stolen that comic. Besides, he knows he's got a poor reputation, he knows he'd be Suspect No.1 in a case like this. He'd be a fool to try something.'

'I dunno,' I muttered. I suddenly remembered those wooden display boxes in Rippa's shop. I'd wondered why they seemed half empty. And now, a specific question came to mind: 'Has Rippa been selling a lot of his stock recently?'

Izzy flicked back through her print-outs. 'He's sold loads of stuff in the past couple of months, yes. And by the looks of it, he's not bought very much.'

Hmm . . .

'I still think there are better suspects elsewhere,' said Izzy. 'What about Ed's dad, for example? He had easy access to the safe.'

I snapped my fingers. 'Aha! He has a shop! He could be in debt; he could have all kinds of money problems!'

'I'm way ahead of you,' said Izzy quietly, with a smug smile, plucking a sheet from the middle of her print-outs. 'I've already checked.'

'Aha!' I cried. 'What a fool I've been not to see it at once! Ed's dad is in financial trouble! He sees the comic book in the safe! He spots a way to clear his debts! He takes the comic! He sells it! Suddenly, his money worries are over! Am I right? Am I right?'

'No.'

'Oh.'

'His shop's doing really well, actually. Has been for years.'

'Oh. Another theory blown out of the water, then.'

'Looks like it,' said Izzy, doing a slow spin in her swivel chair. 'But I still think Ed's dad a more likely suspect than Rippa. Face it, Saxby, this could just be the case that beats you.'

She eyed me with a sly smile.

'Never,' I said, eyeing her without so much as a hint of a sly smile. 'Nobody gets the better of Saxby Smart.'

A Page From My Notebook

Fact: If Rippa DOES have the stolen comic, he certainly isn't trying to sell it.

Question: Has he stolen it simply to keep it? Possibly, but Izzy says he's never bought or sold any issues of THE TOMB OF DEATH, ever. Which implies he's not actually a fan of those comics. So why steal it to keep?

Fact: Rippa's been selling a lot of other comics recently, but he's not been buying much.

Question: Why? Does he need money for something? If so, what?

Question: Is Izzy right? Does Ed's dad have something to do with this, something I haven't spotted so far?

Problem: If Ed's dad IS involved, I'm going to be stirring up all kinds of trouble – Ed and Charlie won't be pleased to discover the identity of the thief!

Problem: What AM I going to do about my Thinking Chair? That rip is still getting worse. And I'm not going near that sticky tape again!

CHAPTER SIX

AT SCHOOL THE NEXT DAY, the case took a decisive turn. And a very unexpected turn it was too!

For most of the morning, I found it hard to concentrate on lessons. Which is normal when we're doing maths, because maths is certainly not my best subject. But today, I was finding it particularly hard to concentrate because of the problems surrounding that comic book. The crime *seemed* impossible, and yet it had happened. The suspects *seemed* to be in the clear, and yet someone must have —

'Saxby Smart?' called Mrs Penzler, our form teacher.

'Er, sorry?' I blinked.

'Are you with us today, Saxby?' snapped Mrs Penzler. The rest of the class giggled quietly. Even Muddy! I glared at him and he pulled a big cheesy grin at me.

'Give us the answer to question three, Saxby!' cried Mrs Penzler.

I hadn't the faintest idea what she was talking about. However, Mrs Penzler is a no-nonsense teacher, and she likes definite answers, so I gave her the most definite answer that came into my head.

'Fourteen,' I said. Definitely.

'It's two point two,' said Mrs Penzler, with a bemused look on her face. 'See me afterwards, and I'll go over this topic with you. Again.'

I sighed and settled down to untangling the jumble of numbers on the page in front of me. I tried hard to follow the rest of the maths lesson, but to be honest I found it about as easy as eating custard with chopsticks. My spirits perked up when the bell went for lunch break, and then they slumped back down again when I remembered my after-lesson appointment with Mrs Penzler. However, my ten-minute chat with her had two *very* important effects.

Effect No. 1: 'Oh I seeeee!' I finally got what she'd been on about all lesson. It was as if the chopsticks had been replaced with a spoon!

Effect No. 2: It made me late for dinner. Which made me late for what I had to do *after* dinner (namely helping to put up a display of artwork outside the school office). Which meant I was standing outside the office when Charlie Foster turned up. If I hadn't been late I'd have missed him entirely.

He was carrying his school bag, and clearly hadn't expected to see me. He gave me a kind of nervous nod and a 'Hello' and went into the office, where he was out of sight and out of earshot.

The art display was just about finished. The two other kids on display duty went back to their classrooms, leaving me to pin up the last couple of labels (*A Map of the Town by 4B* and *By Timmy Liggins of 2L* – Miss Bennett says 'Lovely work, Timmy, well done'. I mean, yeurch!).

A few seconds after Charlie had entered the office, Mrs McEwan the school secretary hurried out. She click-clunked on her tottering high heels over to the staff room, her whole body swaying back and forth on her chunky bare legs.

Kids weren't normally allowed in the office on their own. It occurred to me that Charlie had sent her off on some urgent errand to get her out of the way. I stepped out of sight, behind the display boards. Something was going on.

From inside the office came a loud whirring noise. Then Charlie emerged, still carrying his bag. He had a look about him that could only be described as gleeful. Something in that office had made him very happy indeed.

As soon as he'd gone, I emerged from my hiding place and nipped into the office myself. If I was found in here without good reason, I could be in big trouble. I needed to identify what Charlie had been doing, and fast.

Suddenly, I heard the click-clunk of those high heels, heading back this way! I had time to look in *one* place only, and I had a choice of:

- Mrs McEwan's desk and the heap of stuff on it
- The bin beneath the desk
- The cupboard under the window
- The big paper shredder beside the cupboard
- A box of just-delivered stationery
- The office computer perched on its trolley

The choice was actually quite a simple one. Have you spotted it?

I went straight to the paper shredder. What else would have made that loud whirring noise I'd heard? (Well, unless Charlie had suddenly started doing machinery impressions in his spare time . . . or the computer needed some serious repair work . . .)

'Charlie Foster, you cheeky little so-and-so!' cried Mrs McEwan, clattering back into the room. 'Mrs Penzler does *not* need an emergency box of paper clips, and —'

She stared at me. I think, just for a second, she thought Charlie had suddenly mutated into a different kid.

'I've been sent to empty the shredder,' I lied quickly, unhooking the big plastic sack beneath the machine.

'Oh,' said Mrs McEwan. 'Thank you. If you see Charlie Foster, tell him he's a cheeky little so-and-so.'

'I will,' I said, dragging the sack out of the office.

I took the sack over to the recycling box outside the staff room. I opened it carefully and peered inside. Most of the shreds were plain white strips of paper, but sitting in amongst them were thin slices of something else. I picked up a handful.

These shreds were a browny-white, with multi-coloured bits. The paper felt thin and soft between my fingers. I lifted it to my nose. There was a dusty smell, a smell I'd smelled once before. With a sudden feeling in my stomach as if it had been tied to a giant boulder and thrown off a cliff, I realised what Charlie had been doing.

Have you worked it out too?

He'd just shredded *The Tomb of Death*.

I gasped. Out loud. I flopped. On to the floor. Charlie Foster had just shredded a comic book worth . . . I gasped again.

So *Charlie* had stolen the comic? I could hardly believe it. A dozen enormous questions suddenly popped into my head, most of them beginning with 'Hang on a minute, how on earth . . .?'

Mrs Penzler appeared out of the staff room and loomed over me. 'If you're emptying that sack, then get it emptied and run along to class. Honestly, Saxby, you're in a world of your own today!'

I pulled the remains of the comic out of the sack, and stuffed them into my pockets.

There *had* to be more to this than I was seeing. There just *had* to be. As soon as school was over, I hurried home to my Thinking Chair. Sitting down carefully so as not to make the rip on the arm any worse, I settled down with my notebook, my sharpest pencil and my brain cells.

A Page From My Notebook

Problem: OK, assuming Charlie is the thief, he must have opened the safe. Which means he must have known the combination. How?

Fact: Only Ed and his parents know the combination. They all say they've never told anyone what that combination is. And even if they HAD told Charlie, they'd have no reason to hide the fact.

Conclusion: Charlie FOUND OUT the combination.

Question: How? Certainly not by sneakily watching someone – Ed made it clear that angle was covered!

Problem: Sure, Charlie would be in huge trouble for stealing the comic. But why DESTROY it? An immensely valuable item like that? He'd be in FAR worse trouble by destroying it. Something about this simply DOES NOT add up.

CHAPTER
SEVEN

THE FOLLOWING DAY, SATURDAY, I asked two specific questions. The answers to those two questions finally gave me the key to the entire case.

The first question was one I asked Izzy. I phoned her up and said: 'Safes. Like the one the Fosters have got. Can you set your own combination for them, or do they come with one that you can't change?'

Ten minutes later, she called me back. 'Most of them have a user-set combination. You can use whatever numbers you like. Most people use something memorable, like a birthday or their house number.'

Aha!

The second question came a little later. This time, I phoned Ed Foster. I said: 'I have something here I'd like you to look at.'

He said: 'No problem, I'll come over straight away.'

Twenty minutes later, a clapped-out old banger of a car chugged and shuddered on to the small paved drive in front of my house. I suppose it made sense that a bloke as scruffy as Ed Foster should have a seriously rubbish car like that. Owner and vehicle in perfect harmony.

Unfortunately, Ed had brought Charlie with him. I'd been hoping he wouldn't, but it was too late now. I'd just have to risk it.

This whole meeting was a risk. I needed to show Ed some of the shredded remains of the comic. I was hoping he wouldn't realise exactly what it was I was showing him.

Ed and Charlie came out to my shed. I took just two of the shreds out of my filing cabinet, as Ed perched on my desk. The moment Charlie saw them, he started to shuffle nervously. He realised at once that I must have followed him into the school office. I tried not to give away the fact that I knew that he knew that I knew what these shreds were. I told myself to play it cool.

So now, here comes that vital second question. 'What can you tell me about these?' I asked Ed, handing him the two shreds.

He frowned, then raised his eyebrows. 'Well, they're shredded paper,' he said.

46

My heart was thumping. I needed to establish the age of these shreds. It was central to the whole case. I also needed to choose my words very, very carefully, or I'd have a gibbering wreck of a comic collector on my hands. 'I mean, can you tell me anything about the paper? I only ask because you know a lot about whether some types of paper are old or new.'

Ed examined the shreds up close, turning to hold them up to the light coming through the shed's perspex window. 'Well, this could be standard comic book stock,' he said at last. 'You see the way the coloured ink there is printed in tiny dots? That was certainly what you'd see on older comics.'

I glanced over at Charlie. He'd gone as pale as a ghost in a snowstorm.

'So . . . the paper . . . itself . . .' I said.

'Oh, that's not old,' he said confidently.

I snapped to attention. 'It's not? That's *not* from a very old comic book?'

'No way,' said Ed. 'What on earth makes you think it is? No, if you put old pulp paper through a modern shredder, you end up with a load of little bits, not neat shreds like this. I told you, that old paper is really delicate.'

Aha Number Two!

And it wasn't the 'aha' I'd been expecting. The age of

47

that paper was indeed central to the whole case, but in a way I hadn't quite foreseen. Suddenly, the theories I'd been working on in my head needed to be reversed.

'That's it!' I declared. 'I've solved the case!'

'Really?' cried Ed, grinning. 'So where's my comic book?'

Charlie had turned almost see-through, he was so pale. If he hadn't been leaning on the lawnmower in the corner of the shed, I think he'd have fallen over.

'I'll explain everything when we get to Rippa's shop,' I said.

'It's closed today,' said Ed.

'Why?'

'He's going to America,' said Ed.

'Why?'

'The International Comics Convention in Los Angeles,' said Ed. 'It starts tomorrow.'

Now it was my turn to go pale. I leaned against my Thinking Chair to stop myself falling over.

'Of course,' I gasped. '*That's* what he's been saving up for.'

'Sure, it's an expensive trip,' shrugged Ed. 'Are you telling me *he's* got my comic?'

I nodded. Charlie stared at me, open-mouthed with relief.

'Right!' declared Ed. 'When he gets back, I'll —'

'No, you don't understand!' I cried. 'We have to stop him going, or you'll never see that comic again!'

'Impossible,' wailed Ed. 'If the flight hasn't already gone, it'll be going soon.'

'What about your car?' I said. 'It's only twenty miles to the airport from here.'

'Impossible,' wailed Ed. 'The radiator's bust. It's got a leak that needs to be sealed. At the moment, that car's got a range of about three miles, at most. How about the bus? Or a taxi?'

'Too slow,' I said. 'We need to get there *now*!'

Charlie slid to the shed floor with a bump. 'That's it, then,' he said mournfully. 'It's gone. Rippa's won.'

Ed let out a yelp of anger and panic. I looked around quickly. There had to be something we could do. There had to be some way to fix that car.

And as I looked around at the contents of my shed, an idea struck me. There was something here that had been giving me no end of trouble, but which might, just, make a temporary seal for the car's radiator.

Think back . . .

'This!' I cried, snatching up the reel of super-tough heavy-duty repair tape with which I'd been trying to fix my Thinking Chair. *Guaranteed 100% Bonding Power!* it says!'

Ed took the reel from me. 'Brilliant,' he said.

The three of us raced out to the car. Ed hurriedly refilled the car's radiator from the plastic bottle of water he was carrying around in the boot, and taped up the leak.

'So, Saxby,' said Charlie quietly. 'How exactly did Rippa steal the comic?'

Ed jumped into the driving seat. 'Yeh!' he cried, 'I want to know that too!'

'I'll explain on the way,' I said. 'Now *move!*'

We buckled up as Ed shifted the car into reverse and it lurched around in a semicircle. With tyres screeching like a fast getaway in a movie, the car bounded for the main road.

'Well?' said Ed, as he drove round a sharp bend and headed for the sliproad that joined on to the motorway.

'Well,' I said, watching the grass verge zip past at a frightening speed, and wishing I hadn't been quite so insistent on getting there as fast as possible, 'the thing is, what I didn't realise for ages is that there were *two* thefts here, not one.'

'Two?' said Ed, manoeuvring the car on to the motorway and revving up to a needle's width below the speed limit.

'Yes,' I said. 'The first happened because the thief saw a chance and took it. The second was carefully planned. OK, let's consider the second one first. Ed, do you have a firm hold of that steering wheel?'

'Yes, why?' said Ed.

'Because I've got to tell you that the second crime was done by Charlie.'

'What?' yelled Ed. He whizzed the car into the fast lane and we all swung from side to side. Charlie buried his face in his hands.

'Charlie Foster, you thieving little pipsqueak, I'll —' cried Ed.

'Pack it in!' I cried. 'You just concentrate on driving! Yes, Charlie did it, but hear me out. He didn't intend any harm. He only wanted to borrow the comic for a while. Am I right, Charlie?'

'Yes,' mumbled Charlie from behind his hands. 'I'm sorry, Ed, really. I wish I'd never even heard of that comic.'

'You'll wish you'd never heard of me!' cried Ed. 'Did you give my comic to Rippa? Is that it?'

'No!' cried Charlie.

'I told you, Charlie's was the second crime,' I said. 'It happened like this. Some time ago, you banned Charlie from your entire collection. Now, naturally, Charlie felt a bit miffed by that. After all, the incident with the jam was an accident. Right, Charlie?'

'Right,' mumbled Charlie from behind his hands.

'But, naturally, he was very curious to see *The Tomb of Death*. Your pride and joy. The most valuable collector's item he was ever likely to set eyes on. But it was locked away in the safe.

'Now, Charlie here is a brighter spark than you give him credit for. He might not have known the combination to the safe, but he could work it out. He realised that you and your dad would have set the combination to something memorable. A significant date, a phone number . . . Right, Charlie?'

'Mum's birthday,' mumbled Charlie.

Ed glanced at Charlie a couple of times in his rear-view mirror. 'How did you know that?'

'He didn't, at first,' I said. 'Over several days, when nobody was about, he tried various combinations. Until he found the right one, last Sunday night. So he opened the safe and took out the comic. He only wanted to take a look at it, to read it and see what all the fuss was about. He had every intention of putting it straight back. But almost as soon as he took it out of the safe, he realised that he was in a whole world of doo-doo.'

'Too right,' muttered Ed.

'Ed! Just listen to me,' I said. The car wove ahead, overtaking a lorry and changing lanes to pull away from a chunky people carrier filled with fighting toddlers.

'As soon as Charlie looked through the comic, he realised it was fake. A dummy. A very good one, but a fake none the less.'

'A *what*?' yelled Ed. 'Rubbish! I know every square millimetre of that comic! Do you think I can't tell a fake when I see one?'

'We'll get to that,' I said. 'Keep your eyes on the road! What Charlie took from the safe was not the real *Tomb of Death*. And when he realised that, he panicked. He had no idea what had happened to the real one. Would you think he'd taken it? Who *had* taken it? Had it always been a dummy? Were *you* hiding something?

'He didn't know what to do. OK, with a bit more thought on his part, or by being honest from the start, things might have turned out better. But he was scared; he knew you'd be furious. For a start, there was nothing he could say without having to admit that he'd got into the safe. And he reckoned he'd be in enough trouble for that, let alone whatever might happen because the comic was a fake.

'The point is, while he dithered over what to do, the safe was reopened and the comic was seen to be missing. Then you, Ed, told him to come and see me. Which, reluctantly, he did. And all this time, he was hiding the fake comic away.

'With Saxby Smart on the case, Charlie realised it was only a matter of time before he was found out. Which is true. He still had the fake comic in his school bag. So he went to the office, distracted the school secretary and shredded the fake. Now, at least, when suspicion pointed towards him, there was no physical evidence left.'

'Wait a minute,' said Charlie, finally uncovering his face. 'When you gave Ed those shreds of paper, you thought they might be the real comic, didn't you?'

'Ummmm,' I said, 'yes, but, anyway, moving on —'

'As if I'd do that,' muttered Charlie.

'Moving on,' I said quickly. 'We come to the *first* theft. The theft of the *real Tomb of Death*.'

'By Rippa,' said Ed.

'By Rippa,' I nodded. 'Izzy's research, and my own observations, had shown Rippa to be a dodgy dealer in more ways than one. He'd already tried to pass off a facsimile edition comic as the genuine article. He'd nearly succeeded too. So what more logical step for him than to go one better, and produce a really convincing fake, one that only an expert would spot? And why not aim high? Why not go for one of the most valuable comics there is? *The Tomb of Death* Issue 1.

'From various published sources, he could reproduce the comic's covers and inside pages. And there was a local dealer he knew, Ed Foster, who actually *had* a copy. If he played his cards right, he could go along and take a look at the real thing, to make sure that his fake was as perfect as possible.

'The trouble was, he didn't have a good reputation in the trade. He decided that, once his fake was ready, he'd travel to one of the big American trade fairs, where he wasn't known, and sell it there. In a huge place like America, the selling of a super-valuable comic book wouldn't attract quite the same attention it would over here. So he worked away at his fake, and he managed to get you, Ed, to show him the real comic, for comparison. You said he had some catalogues with him when he came to your house?'

'Yes,' said Ed.

'And tucked inside one of them, was his carefully made forgery. He only intended to get a close look at your comic. He knew you'd never allow him to borrow it, or anything like that. But when the doorbell went, and he was left alone in that room, he spotted the opportunity of a lifetime. Purely by luck, his forgery was to hand, and he made a snap decision. While you were gone, just for a few seconds, he swapped the real comic for his fake. He gambled that when you came back in, you'd put the comic in the safe straight away, without examining it closely. And that's exactly what you did. You assumed that was your comic back in its plastic case. It wasn't. Rippa slipped the real *Tomb of Death* in amongst his catalogues, and he walked out with it, right under your nose.'

'But he must have known I'd spot the forgery eventually,' said Ed.

'Oh, eventually, yes,' I said. 'But he knew you never, ever normally took that comic out of the safe, let alone out of its protective case. It might have stayed in there for months, or even years, before being discovered. I said to you when I examined the safe that only a pretty stupid and desperate thief would try to snatch that comic, but I was wrong. Rippa took huge risks, but he wasn't daft.

'Think about it. If you, months or even years later, discovered the fake, and even if you linked the fake to Rippa, what actual evidence would you have? None. Even if you told the world, and ruined Rippa's reputation for good, he'd hardly mind, would he? He'd have sold the real comic and be living off a mountain of cash.

'He took a risk, and it appeared to pay off. The only problem was, he now had a genuine *Tomb of Death* and needed to get rid of it. He needed money to finance his trip to America, so he started selling off stock from his shop. He's been selling loads and buying little, to make sure he had enough money to make the earliest trip to America he could. Today. And once he'd sold the comic . . .'

'. . . No evidence again,' said Ed, grinding his teeth. 'Unless I spent a fortune following the comic around America and tracking its sale.'

'Right,' I said.

Ed flicked the indicator and the car sped towards the exit off the motorway. By the little clock that was Blu-tacked to the dashboard, the time was 3.22 p.m.

It was 3.27 p.m. when we raced into the car park opposite the main entrance to the airport. Charlie and I hurried over to the terminal building while Ed hunted through the rubbish in the car's glove compartment for some change to pay for parking.

3.28 p.m. The glass doors slid aside and Charlie and I stepped into a swirling river of people, trolleys and baggage. Tugging at Charlie's sleeve to get him to follow me, I headed straight for the enormous Departures screen, hanging above a nearby coffee stall.

3.29 p.m. 'Let's see, let's see,' I muttered. 'Look for

LAX. That's Los Angeles. No, wait, that's arrivals. C'mon, c'mon, c'mon, LAX, LAX, LAX . . . I can't see it. Wait, the screen's changing . . .'

Charlie poked his head into view. 'There's one flight to LA today; passengers have just been called to the departure lounge, over there, Gate 22B.'

I glanced back and forth between him and the screen. 'That's genius. How did you work that out?'

'I asked that air stewardess over there.'

'Ah, right,' I said, nodding a thank you to a woman in a ghastly green uniform.

3.30 p.m.

We sped up a short staircase and across a wide area covered in shiny floor tiles and bolted-down seats. The departure lounge was directly ahead of us. Passengers were lining up at a row of scanners, ready to have their bags checked.

And there was Rippa! He was facing away from us, a holdall in one hand and a pack of sandwiches in the other. He was almost at the front of the queue.

'He hasn't seen us,' said Charlie.

'But if he gets past those scanners, he's gone!' I said. 'Airport security means we won't be able to follow him any further!'

We hurried towards him, worried in case we drew

attention to ourselves. If he spotted us now, all he'd have to do is leave the queue and lose himself in the crowd.

'Whatever you do,' I whispered, 'don't run. Don't cause anyone in that queue to look round.'

Suddenly, Ed overtook us, running like his bum was on fire, heading directly for Rippa. Charlie and I both pulled yeeargh-faces.

But it was almost too late. Rippa was at the head of the queue. In a few seconds, he'd be through the scanners. Even at full speed, Ed wouldn't reach him in time!

'How can we stop him?' wailed Charlie.

For a split second, my mind went blank. But then I had a brilliant idea.

'Oi!' I shouted, at the top of my voice. 'Oi! Tarquin!'

The sound echoed off the flickering screens and the shiny floor. As one, every last person in sight turned to stare at me. Rippa, with a face like a mad bull, spun on his heels. Without a moment's thought, he flung his pack of sandwiches directly at me, his mouth pulled into a wedge-shaped sneer. The sandwiches bounced and skidded to a halt at my feet.

'So it's true,' I said. 'He really does throw things at people who call him that.'

Rippa's pause gave Ed just enough time to reach him. Rippa almost made a run for it, but Ed took a firm hold of his arm and dragged him out of the queue.

'Open it, please,' said Ed, pointing to Rippa's holdall.

With his free hand, and a grunting sigh, Rippa unzipped the holdall. Nestled inside, between some scrunched-up T-shirts and a spare pair of jeans, was a cardboard folder. Inside the folder was Issue 1 of *The Tomb of Death*.

'How did you know?' grunted Rippa.

'I didn't,' said Ed. He pointed to me. 'He did.'

'And who are you?' sniffed Rippa, looking me up and down. 'Sherlock bloomin' Holmes?'

'No,' I said with a smile. 'My name is Saxby Smart.'

On the way home, Charlie expected to get one giant, economy-sized telling-off from his brother, but it seemed that Ed was a changed man. 'I shouldn't have been so tough on you over the jam, Charlie,' he said, as the car chugged back into town. 'If I'd been less crabby, you might have come straight to me in the first place. Sorry.'

'Does that mean I can read your collection?' said Charlie excitedly.

Ed said nothing for a while. 'Dunno,' he mumbled eventually. 'I'll think about it.'

Once I was home, I retreated to my shed. I made some notes on the case, and then I settled back in my Thinking

Chair. There was a slight ripping sound from the arm. I sighed, and finally had to admit to myself that even a simple repair job like that was beyond me. I'd call my friend Muddy in the morning, I decided. Get a professional in.

Case closed.

CASE FILE FIVE:

THE TREASURE OF DEAD MAN'S LANE

CHAPTER ONE

'OOOH DEAR,' SAID MUDDY. 'Ooooh dear, oh dear, oh dear. Oooooooh dear.'

'Yeh, OK,' I said grumpily. 'Can you fix it?'

Muddy examined the rip in the arm of my Thinking Chair, prodding it with a grimy finger. 'Ooooh dear. Yup, that's fixable. Should have called me in earlier, though, Saxby. You've let this develop into quite a nasty little tear.'

'I can do without the lecture, thanks,' I said. 'I did try to fix it myself, you know.'

'Yeh, I can tell,' muttered Muddy, doing a bit more prodding. 'What a botch-up. Sticky tape, was it?'

'Just get on with it,' I grumbled. 'Stop enjoying yourself.'

My great friend George 'Muddy' Whitehouse is a genius when it comes to practical and mechanical things. He goes around looking like he's been dragged through an assortment of puddles and ditches, but there's nobody at St Egbert's School who's more skilled at mending stuff. In less than ten minutes, there was a neatly glued patch on the arm of my Thinking Chair.

'Leave it for an hour or two before you sit in it,' said Muddy, packing up his toolbox.

'Thanks,' I said. 'You know how important my Thinking Chair is. Do you want to stay for lunch?'

'Can't,' said Muddy, with a gleam of excitement in his eyes. 'I'm going over to The Horror House. I'm getting a guided tour this afternoon.'

'You're joking,' I gasped. 'How? Tellmetellmetellme!' Obviously, I couldn't see my own eyes at that moment, but I'm pretty certain they had a gleam of excitement in them too.

The Horror House was something of a local legend. If any building ever deserved a nickname, it was number 13, Deadman Lane. Imagine a spooky old house in a movie. Then imagine it much spookier than that. Then add a bit more spookiness for extra effect, and you still wouldn't be anywhere close to how utterly creepy this place looked.

It was a large, looming house, with huge bay windows to either side of a squat-shaped front door, from which protruded an ornate, stone-columned porch. There were two upper floors, each with a series of tall, narrow windows that gave an impression of gappy teeth. The roof was sharply angled, topped with a ridge of crested tiles, and a couple of dormers poked out of it, which looked like narrowed eyes above the skull-like grin of the windows below.

Nobody had lived at 13, Deadman Lane for years. The place was boarded up, set back from the road behind a high fence of corrugated metal sheeting. People started calling it The Horror House because of its weird looks, and because it was an ideal reference point if you wanted to give someone directions to the shopping mall ('You go straight past The Horror House and it's left at the traffic lights.').

'But how are you even getting in there?' I said. 'It's all locked and barred.'

'Not since Monday, it's not,' said Muddy, grinning. 'Jack's parents have bought it.'

'Jack Wilson in our class?' I said. 'He kept that quiet.'

'He didn't even know himself until Monday. His mum and dad didn't know if they'd get the money for it. They're going to do it up, and turn it into a hotel. Jack says his dad says they're up to their eyeballs in debt until they can renovate the whole place. The electrics haven't been updated since 1955, and it's still got a heating system dated 1937. A broken heating system, of course.'

'Wow,' I said. 'I take it they're getting started straight away?'

'Those heating pipes got taken out on Tuesday,' said Muddy. 'Pity. I'd love to get my hands on a bit of vintage machinery like that. They've been ripping stuff out every day. Which is lucky, really, because otherwise they wouldn't have found the secret parchment.'

'Secret parchment?' I said, intrigued.

'Oh, Jack says his dad says it's not a real one. But it sounds like fun, all the same. It claims there's treasure hidden somewhere in that house.'

I steered Muddy out of the shed and into the house. 'I want to hear more about this mysterious parchment,' I said. 'You've changed your mind, you're staying for lunch after all.'

CHAPTER
TWO

AS MUDDY AND I SAT at the kitchen table, scoffing our beans on toast, he told me about the parchment.

'Jack and his dad found it the other day,' said Muddy, piling up beans on his fork. 'They were ripping out some old wooden wall panels in one of the upstairs rooms. This panelling had been put in when the house was built, about two hundred years ago, you can tell by looking at the wall behind, apparently. But the damp had recently got to it, and it was past saving. Anyway, they were stacking up all these big pieces of wood, and Jack suddenly noticed a sheet of paper, wedged into a sort of slot at the back of one of the panels.'

'A sort of slot?' I said.

'Jack's dad took a look at it,' said Muddy. 'There was a

removable section in that panel, quite low down, behind a spot they'd removed a radiator from. A kind of hidden storage box, no bigger than a school lunch box. They'd never have found it without removing all those panels from the wall.'

'And this parchment is a treasure map?'

'Yes. Well, it's not so much a map, more a description of where the treasure is. Although apparently this description doesn't make much sense. Anyway, Jack says his dad says it's not as old as it looks. He reckons it was probably put there by the orphans.'

'Orphans?' I said, chewing at a triangle of toast.

'During World War Two, the house was a shelter for kids who'd been orphaned by the bombing. Loads and loads of people have lived in that house over the years. It's only recently that it's been empty and run down.'

'And these orphans made this parchment?' I said.

'That's the theory. It's just the sort of thing a bunch of kids would do, isn't it. They come to live in a spooky old house, and they start making up games about hidden treasure and so forth. This piece of paper must have been left over from their games.'

'And how did they find that hidden compartment?'

Muddy shrugged. 'Just came across it one day, I guess. Then left their treasure map in there by mistake, maybe.

Of course, it might not have been the orphans at all. Could have been kids from the 1960s, or the 1970s or something. The house was still lived in until 1987. Anyway, Jack says his dad says it was most probably the orphans.'

I thought carefully for a minute or two. No, Jack's dad was definitely wrong. Perhaps he was distracted by the huge job he'd taken on, but there was an obvious logical flaw in his theory. From what Muddy had told me so far, I knew that the parchment had to be nearly a century old, at the very least. And I knew that the orphans couldn't possibly have put it there: it was a question of historical events . . .

Have you spotted it?

Muddy had told me that the heating system was dated 1937. He'd also told me that it had only been removed on Tuesday, the secret compartment being behind where a radiator had been fixed. Which meant that during the whole of World War Two, 1939–1945, the orphans couldn't have got to the compartment. In fact, *nobody* could have got to that compartment since 1937, so the parchment had to be at least that old, and possibly much older.

I decided there and then that learning dates in history lessons at school was a useful thing to do after all!

'Come on,' I said. 'Let's take a look at that piece of paper. I think it could be perfectly genuine.'

'Hang on,' called Muddy, as I sped off, 'I haven't finished my beans yet!'

CHAPTER
THREE

'NOW **THAT** IS SPOOKY,' I whispered.

'It's like it's looking back at you,' Muddy replied.

The Horror House stood like a huge, crouching goblin. It was set back from the road, and surrounded by a snarling, overgrown garden. Behind it, we could see the tops of the trees in the wooded area that led down to the local canal. (That wood was equally gloomy, and had an equally sinister nickname: The Hangman's Lair. I solved a very puzzling mystery there once. I might write up my notes on that case one day.)

Number 13 stood well away from the other houses in Deadman Lane, as if it was being snotty and didn't want to talk to its neighbours. The tall sheets of corrugated metal that had fenced the house for as long as I could remember had all been torn down. They were stacked in a huge heap amid the tangle of thistles and thorns that nipped at us as Muddy and I walked up the cracked path to the front door.

Jack Wilson greeted us like an excited puppy. The human equivalent of an excited puppy, I mean. He didn't lick our faces. Or have a tail to wag. Or bark. But you get the idea. Jack was a round, bouncy boy, with a face that always looked as if he'd just got some really good news. He ushered us inside a large, shadowy hallway.

'Wooooww,' gasped Muddy, taking it all in.

'So this is The Horror House,' I said, gazing up at the high ceiling.

'It's revooooolting,' breathed Muddy, eyeing the cracked plaster and the peeling paint and the damp shreds of wallpaper clinging in miserable patches above the high skirting boards.

'Yeh, it's not too good at the moment,' agreed Jack. 'Still, if it was beautifully decorated we'd have been calling it The Lovely House all these years, wouldn't we? Mind out for that floorboard, Saxby, it's rotten. Mum put her foot straight through it yesterday. I laughed till I cried.'

Sounds of heavy-duty machinery were echoing from somewhere upstairs. We picked our way carefully up the wide, curved staircase and waited on the landing until the loud sawing noises stopped and the cloud of dust that was drifting out of one of the bedrooms subsided.

Jack's dad appeared through the dust haze, wielding a huge circular saw. The saw's battered power cable hung from his other hand like a lasso. From the heels of his boots to the bald patch on his head, he was caked in a mixture of sawdust, white emulsion paint and more sawdust.

'Hello,' he said, grinning. 'Watch where you step.'

'The rotten floorboards?' said Muddy.

'No, our rotten cat. Dirty little so-and-so,' said Jack's dad. 'He sees a pile of sawdust and thinks it's a litter tray. S'cuse me, I've got to knock out some old plaster before Jack's mum gets back from the builder's merchant. Then I've got the man from the Planning Department coming. Then I've got to find the broom I left around here somewhere.'

'Yeh, the floor could do with a good sweep,' said Jack.

'No, I was going to whack the cat with it,' muttered Jack's dad. 'Dirty little so-and-so.'

We left Jack's dad to work his way through his To Do list. The sound of a sledgehammer breaking stuff apart followed us along the hallway. As Jack showed us into a large, dusty room overlooking the road, Muddy told him about our earlier discussion.

'You really think that parchment is as old as the

house?' said Jack. Our shoes crunched against the grit that littered the bare floor.

'We know it must pre-date 1937,' I said. 'And if that storage compartment was as well hidden and as precisely sized as Muddy said, then it's quite possible that it was built into the wood panelling specifically to hide that one piece of paper.'

'That's a bit extreme, isn't it?' said Muddy. 'To build a compartment into a wall just for that? If what's written on the paper is *that* secret, why write it down at all? Why not just memorise it?'

'Quite,' said Jack. 'It's a spooky-sounding load of nonsense, which someone made up and hid years and years ago, giggling away to themselves, knowing that someone else would come along and get all excited about it. It really is just gobbledegook. I think you're wrong, Saxby, I think it's a long-lost Victorian practical joke.'

'This is the room you found it in?' I said. It was a large but unremarkable room, with two tall windows – two of those 'teeth' in the front face of the building – and an irregularly-shaped fireplace built into one corner.

'I've got it over here,' said Jack. From off the deep windowsill he fetched a box file, the sort of solid cardboard case you see in offices for keeping papers in. He flipped it open and handed it to me.

Inside was a sheet of thick paper, about thirty centimetres tall and fifteen wide. Its left-hand edge was slightly jagged, the others neatly cut. It was yellowed with age, with brownish spots and blotches here and there across its surface, but it was surprisingly smooth and solid to the touch. Obviously very expensive paper (the exact opposite of the sort encountered in the case of *The Tomb of Death*!).

On the paper, in angular but flowing handwriting, were lines written in black ink, all neatly level on the page. The words had clearly been written with one of those old-fashioned dip-in-the-ink pens: you could see where the ink kept thinning out every few words, then suddenly become thicker again when the pen was dipped. In all it said:

Now, three by itself of eighth, solar revolutions twenty from Bonaparte's fall, and nine, I hereby veil my dark and mighty treasure.

Through its right eye, it sees a bullet-line down half a corner.
Through its left eye, the canvas.
Bisect and again, and lo! the needle's mark, Rome's war-god steps to the circle's edge.

Eastward the sky, westward the earth, northward we go and beneath.

Mirror the prize and see the trees, fall from the glass and feel the soil.

Down, and down, and where the saucer goes, go I.

SM

'Well,' said Jack, reading the paper again over my shoulder, 'I've come across some obscure treasure trails in my time, but that takes the cake! It's gobbledegook. It's a joke, it has to be.'

'It's not gobbledegook,' I said, peering closely at the parchment in the grey light from the window. 'It's simply a complicated puzzle. It leads to this "dark and mighty treasure", I'm sure of it. It's far too elaborate to be nothing more than a practical joke.'

'OK, then, make sense of just one line,' said Jack. 'Show me exactly what one line means, and I'll believe you.'

I read through the words again. They certainly appeared to defy logic! But, assuming that I was right and that they *did* actually mean something, it was possible to make a guess about what the first line might mean. After all, if you were writing an important document, what would you be most likely to put at the top?

'I can tell you the exact date on which this was written,' I said.

'Oh yeh?' said Jack.

'Oh yeh,' I said. 'I just need to check a historical fact.'

I flipped my phone open and called The Fountain of All Knowledge, or Izzy, as she prefers to be called. 'Quick fact-check,' I said. 'Could you look up the date on which Napoleon Bonaparte was finally defeated?'

'Who?' muttered Muddy.

'French bloke. Late eighteenth century, early nineteenth,' I said. 'I think. If I'm remembering what I read in *The Boy's Big Encyclopedia of Facts* correctly.'

There was a click on the line as Izzy returned. 'Battle of Waterloo,' she said. '1815. Is something interesting going on?'

'Something very interesting indeed. I'll get back to you. I may need a lot of background info finding on this one.'

I pocketed my phone, turned to Jack, and pointed out the first line on the treasure 'map', up to the bit that said 'my dark and mighty treasure'.

'There's the date,' I said.

My maths is generally about as strong as a soggy tissue, but with a bit of lateral thinking and a bit of simple maths I could see that the first part of the sentence was a date and a month. And then, using a bit of maths and a bit of general science knowledge, I could see that the second part of the sentence gave a year.

Can you work it out?

'This was written on 9 August 1844,' I said.

Now, three by itself of eighth, solar revolutions twenty from Bonaparte's fall, and nine . . .

'Three by itself of eighth,' I said. 'Our whoever-it-was is putting the date at the top of his work. "Three by itself" could be simply the number three, on its own? Not if this is meant to be a puzzle! That would be far too easy. No, I think it's three *times* itself, three times three. Nine. Of course, I can't be *sure* of that, but I reckon it's likely. And "of eighth"? Of the eighth month? August.'

'Hmm, s'pose so,' said Jack doubtfully.

'Next, the year. "Solar revolutions"? Well, one revolution of the sun means one year, right? We did that in science ages ago, yes? So, twenty years from "Bonaparte's fall", and then another nine. Napoleon was defeated in 1815, add twenty-nine and you get 1844.'

'Why not take away twenty-nine?' said Muddy.

'Because you'd be dating your document *before* "Bonaparte's fall",' said Jack, 'and that wouldn't make sense, because you wouldn't know about it.'

'Right,' I said. 'Do you believe me now? These words *do* mean something. I think they lead to something important.'

'I think you could be right after all,' whispered Jack.

'Maybe there's a chest full of gold,' said Muddy. 'A pirate's hoard or something.'

'I think 1844's a bit late for pirates,' I said. 'But you never know.'

We stared at each other with our eyes boggling, our jaws dropping and our feet skipping about as if we were a bunch of over-excited horses. There was a secret treasure hidden in The Horror House, a treasure that had been hidden for many years, and we were going to find it!

A Page From My Notebook

What can I deduce about that parchment or, rather, the person who wrote it? He (or she) . . .

1. . . . was a neat and tidy sort of person. The parchment was written in those straight, even lines, carefully set out on the page. BUT! What is the significance of that tear along the left-hand side? Was the paper ripped out of something? Or was something removed from it?

2. . . . was clever, to compose such an obviously complex set of riddles.

3. . . . probably had reason to be fearful. Otherwise, why go to such lengths to conceal this treasure? But fearful of what? Of whom? And why? If the treasure is stolen gold, or such like, then the answers are obvious. But is that the whole story?

4. . . . had the initials SM!

Problem: Muddy's got a good point – if the treasure was such a secret, why create a trail to it at all? Why not simply commit the location of the treasure to memory?

Answer: He/she MUST have intended to pass the treasure on.

Problem: Why pass it on using such a strange method?

Answer: The way the 'map' is written MUST have been designed to be understandable to whoever it was intended for, BUT to seem obscure gobbledegook to whoever it WASN'T meant for. That might be important. Must think about that some more.

CHAPTER
FOUR

THE NEXT DAY WAS SATURDAY. Muddy and I arrived back at the house for 9 a.m., ready for a solid day's fortune-hunting. Muddy brought along a rucksack full of assorted gadgets of his own design. I wasn't sure how useful the *Whitehouse Silent Alarm Mark II* or the *Whitehouse Personal Reversing Mirror* might turn out to be, but I thought that having a few tools to hand was a good idea all the same.

Izzy turned up at quarter past nine. I'd called her back the night before and given her the full story, and also sent her a copy of the treasure trail. Jack's parents had been given a pile of old documents and papers when they'd bought the house: legal stuff, plans of where the drains went, a certificate from when the plumbing was installed, all that sort of stuff. None of it was of help in deciphering the parchment, and none of it recorded anything earlier than 1900. So I was counting on Izzy to come up trumps!

Us boys were all in tatty jeans and sweatshirts, because we were expecting to get as dusty as Jack's dad, but Izzy turned up in her usual out-of-school look, all glittery curls and snazzy colours.

'You'll ruin those trousers,' I said, raising an eyebrow.

'I'm not staying,' said Izzy. 'I only came over to get a closer look at The Horror House. I've got *loads* of leads for information, but I need to go to the library and search through local records. Wow, this place is a dump.'

'A dump with hidden treasure in it,' corrected Muddy.

'A dump that *might* have hidden treasure in it,' corrected Jack.

We trudged across the hallway, our boots kicking up delicate clouds of plaster dust. Various thumps and clanks and ka-chuggs echoed from elsewhere: Jack's mum was busy shovelling sand into the hired cement mixer in the back garden, and Jack's dad was busy chasing the cat. As we all sat at the bottom of the staircase, I took out the photocopy of the parchment I'd made and read through it for the thirty-seventh time.

'What have you got so far?' I said to Izzy.

Izzy plucked a print-out from inside the plastic folder she was carrying. 'This house was built in 1837, by a man called Silas Middlewich.'

'SM!' said Muddy.

'Originally, it was a workhouse, a kind of half-prison where poor people ended up when they had nowhere left to go. They were terrible places. This street was originally called Mill Lane, but once the workhouse was here, everyone started calling it Dead Man's Lane, because it was said that nobody left here alive.'

'And over time, Dead Man's Lane became Deadman Lane,' I said.

Izzy nodded. 'I still have a lot of research to do on this Silas Middlewich, but it seems he was an A-grade Mr Nasty. He packed more and more people into this place and forced them to work for him until he was the richest man in the district. He died in 1845; it's said he was murdered by one of his workers, a woman called Martha Humble. Apparently he'd swindled her husband.'

'Nice guy,' I muttered.

'Still, someone like that is exactly the sort of person who might have hidden his ill-gotten gains in a secret stash,' said Muddy excitedly.

I wasn't so sure. I thought back to my notes, about deductions that could be made from the parchment.

Something didn't add up there.

'You could be right,' said Izzy. 'But there's a vital point you're all missing. Saxby's theory about that secret compartment must be wrong.'

'I beg your pardon?' I said, looking up suddenly.

'The wall panelling was built at the same time as the house. Which we now know was 1837. But you've worked out that the parchment is dated 1844. So the compartment was there for seven years, empty. Doesn't make sense.'

'Hmm,' I said, getting a sinking feeling. 'I don't get it. That compartment was the perfect size for the parchment in height and width.'

'Perhaps,' said Muddy, 'the compartment was originally used to hide the treasure, but then it got moved?'

'No,' I said. 'The compartment was only a few centimetres deep. Not big enough.'

'Plus,' said Izzy, in a way which added I-don't-want-to-put-another-spanner-in-the-works-*but* . . . 'why would someone like Middlewich leave a treasure trail for someone to follow? If he was as nasty as his reputation suggests, he wouldn't want anyone getting their hands on his cash, would he?'

'Ugh! Well, that's a great start,' said Jack. 'You really got my hopes up there, Saxby.'

I held up a hand for quiet. I was trying to think. What Izzy had just said was absolutely right. There was another layer of mystery here: there was a strange difference between what I had worked out about the parchment, and what Izzy had found out about this Silas Middlewich. We'd found a weird gap in history!

One thing was for sure. It was now even more vital that we decipher the parchment. There were more secrets involved in this matter than buried treasure alone.

I jumped to my feet. 'Muddy, Jack, we're getting to work on the parchment, right now. Izzy, to the library. Find out all you can. Get back to us as soon as possible.'

CHAPTER FIVE

'OK, THE FIRST LINE IS THE DATE, let's work on the second,' I said.

Through it's right eye, it sees a bullet–line down half a corner . . .

'What's "it"?' said Muddy.

'What's half a corner?' said Jack.

'If I'm correctly following Silas Middlewich's way of working,' I said, 'half a corner probably means half a right angle. Forty-five degrees. Basic maths again.'

'What's "it"?' said Muddy.

'So, by a bullet-line, do you think he just means a straight line?' said Jack. 'The line that a bullet would take?'

'I think that's highly likely,' I said.

'Hellooooo?' said Muddy. 'What's "it"? And where's its right eye?'

'I haven't the faintest idea,' said Jack.

'Neither have I.' I shrugged. But suddenly, the answer hit me harder than a brick wrapped in concrete. My mind flashed back to the previous day, when Muddy and I had arrived in Deadman Lane. Immediately, I knew exactly where this eye was, and what it belonged to.

Have you spotted it?

I dashed outside, the others following. At the edge of the pavement, I turned and pointed up at the windows.

'It's the house itself!' I said. 'Remember the way it seems to have a face? That window, up there, poking out of the roof. The house's right eye!'

'Bingo!' cried Jack. 'But . . . that's its left eye.'

'No, the parchment says "it sees a bullet-line". *It* does the seeing. From the house's point of view, *that*'s its right eye.'

We dashed back inside, and up to the room with the 'right eye' for a window. It was a small, cobweb-covered room, with a sharply angled ceiling and two floorboards missing from one corner.

'Now, a straight line from the window, looking down at a forty-five degree angle,' I said.

Muddy almost yelped with excitement. From his rucksack he produced an ordinary protractor and the viewfinder mechanism from an old camera, on to which he'd stencilled the words *FlixiScope Model B*.

'Will this help?' he said.

'Not pin-point accurate, but it'll do,' I said.

Muddy held the protractor, Jack judged the angle and, screwing up one eye, I looked through the viewfinder. Directly in the line of its crosshairs was an empty paper sack marked *DIY Warehouse Readymix Concrete*, which must have been blown around the side of the house and got caught in the front garden.

'We're in luck,' I said. 'That bag marks the correct spot.'

We dashed back outside. By now I was getting out of breath, and telling myself I really ought to get more exercise.

We picked our way across the snagging, thorny jungle of a front garden until we found the empty bag. Muddy stood right in the centre of it, exactly where the viewfinder had pointed.

Through its left eye, the canvas.

'OK, Muddy, now look up at the house's left-eye window,' I said. 'What do you see?'

'Nothing,' said Muddy.

'What can "the canvas" be?' said Jack. 'A painting?'

'Possibly,' I said. 'But I think it's more likely to be something else. I doubt the trail would rely on having a particular object put in a particular place.'

'Why?' said Muddy.

'Because something like that could so easily change,' I said. 'You'd only have to move this painting and the whole puzzle would fall apart. Silas Middlewich must be referring to something that probably wouldn't change over time. What *can* you see, Muddy?'

'Nothing. Just the window.'

'And through it?'

'Just the wall opposite.'

'Well, that's it, then!' I cried. 'A big blank wall! You could call that a canvas, couldn't you?'

We dashed back inside again. Now I was *really* getting out of breath and wishing I'd made more effort during PE lessons.

The far wall of the 'left-eye' room was tall and rectangular. The pale yellow paint that covered it was darkened with age around the edges, and there was a slightly lighter, sharply defined patch to one side, where a heavy piece of furniture must have stood for many years.

Bisect and again, and lo! the needle's mark, Rome's war-god steps to the circle's edge.

'Now what's *that* supposed to mean?' said Jack.

'Bisect,' I muttered. 'More maths. That's geometry.'

'Yeh, bisecting means dividing in two, doesn't it?' said Muddy.

'So we're looking for an area of the wall,' said Jack.

'An exact point, rather than an area,' I said. 'It says "the needle's mark". The mark a needle would leave is a point.'

'Right,' said Jack. '"Bisect and again", that must mean we divide it twice. And if we want to find a point, that means we have to draw the lines in opposite directions, so they cross. But how are we supposed to do the dividing? Floor to ceiling? Corner to corner?'

'Doesn't matter,' I said. 'It must mean the dead centre of the wall. Whichever way you halve the wall, top to bottom or corner to corner, you'll get the same thing. The centre.'

Hurriedly, Muddy fetched a ball of string and a marker pen from his bag. Standing on a packing crate, I held one end of the string at the top left corner of the wall, Jack held the other end at the bottom right, and Muddy marked the line. Once the second line was drawn, bottom left to top right, we had our mark!

We stood back from the wall. None of us said anything, but there was a tangible sense of nervous anticipation in the room, an eager thrill of discovery.

Rome's war-god steps to the circle's edge.

'Logically, we must now need to go somewhere from

the centre point we've just marked,' I said. 'And this next line on the parchment implies we go to the edge of a circle. Or at least, I *think* that's what it implies.'

'With the centre point as the centre of the circle?' said Jack.

'But how big a circle?' said Muddy.

We stood there pondering for a few moments. The late morning sunshine threw geometric shapes of light across the wall.

'I wonder if this bit about Rome's war-god is a measurement?' I said, more to myself than the others. 'A measurement of the size of the circle, maybe?'

'Well, the Roman god of war was Mars,' said Jack. 'We know that from doing Ancient Rome in class last year. But we need a number, not a name.'

'The Romans used letters for numbers!' cried Muddy suddenly. 'Is that it?'

'No,' said Jack. 'The only letter in 'Mars' they used was the M, and that equalled one thousand. A thousand of anything would be too big a measurement to fit on the wall.'

'How about the *planet* Mars?' I said. 'Our friend Silas seems to like these little cross-references, doesn't he. Mars is the fourth planet. Hang on, is it? Er . . . Mercury, Venus, Earth . . . yes, Mars is fourth, definitely. There's a possible number.'

'Yeh, but four what?' said Jack. 'What's the unit of measurement? Good grief, look at us, doing maths in our spare time! Mrs Penzler would be delighted!'

'Four . . . "steps", presumably,' I said, frowning. 'Rome's war-god *steps* to the circle's edge.'

'But how big is a step?' said Jack. 'It depends how long your legs are!'

'And how do we walk along the wall to measure them?' said Muddy.

'It can't literally mean steps, as such,' I said. 'Remember, this is a puzzle. The word "step" must translate into our missing unit of measurement somehow. Silas must have wanted to indicate something standard, something that would be meaningful to whoever was meant to follow the trail, something that in 1844 would be —'

I stopped in mid-sentence. My eyes darted to Muddy's rucksack.

'Muddy, have you got a ruler?'

Muddy quickly ferreted around in the bag. He pulled out a round, chunky object and handed it over.

'Muddy,' said Jack, 'that's just a tape measure with a label saying *Whitehouse Measure-Tek 2000* stuck on it!'

'Shut uuuup!' said Muddy. 'It does the job!'

I pulled out a length of the metal measuring tape, and

twisted it over to read the markings printed on its yellow surface.

'Of course, feet and inches!' I cried. 'Old-fashioned feet and inches. We think of everything in metres, don't we? But lots of people still use feet and inches, and people in 1844 wouldn't have used anything else. The measurement is four feet! That's the radius of the circle!'

'Eh?' said Jack.

'I told you, "steps" must indicate a unit of measurement,' I said. 'What do you step with? Feet. Four feet to the circle's edge. Terrible example of word-substitution, but it fits.'

Using the tape measure locked off at the right length, and keeping one end of the tape positioned over the centre point of the wall, we marked out a huge circle.

'Hey, we're really getting somewhere now,' said Muddy with a grin.

'I guess the next line tells us where on the circle to look,' I said. 'What direction to take from the centre.'

Eastward the sky, westward the earth, northward we go and beneath.

'Oh yeh?' said Jack. 'How? The sky isn't east, no matter where you are!'

I was on a roll! I spotted it at once. Standing back, looking at the circle we'd drawn on the wall, I was reminded of a slightly off-centre compass. And suddenly, the answer was obvious.

Can you see it?

'Look at the wall,' I said. 'We're after a direction. "Eastward the sky" it says. Twist the points of the compass so that, as marked on this particular wall, east is up. That places west at the bottom.'

'Towards the earth,' said Muddy. '"Westward the earth".'

Jack groaned and slapped his hand to his face.

'Northward then points left,' I said. 'Follow that to the edge of the circle, and we arrive *here*.' I tapped at the 'northerly' edge of the circle.

'So what does "and beneath" mean?' said Jack. 'Where do we go now?'

'Into the wall,' I said simply. 'If north is to the left, then beneath is thataway.'

'Fantastic!' said Muddy. 'Demolition!'

He rooted around in his rucksack, and pulled out what looked like a metal cylinder fixed into a wire frame.

'I've only just developed this. It doesn't even have a name yet. The digger is pushed forward by this spring, which came out of an old sofa, and when you switch on it starts —'

'Is this some sort of drill?' I said.

'Yup,' said Muddy proudly. 'The lever here adjusts the —'

'Isn't this just the tiniest bit dangerous?' I said.

'Only if you're silly with it,' said Muddy. 'It was designed to cut holes in lawns, for when you want to play golf. But it should work on plaster OK. The only trouble is, the battery pack only lasts for six and a half seconds at the moment. Needs some work.'

Jack and I stood back a little. Then we stood back a little more. Muddy held the wire frame against the wall at the correct spot. Jack and I stood back a little more.

Muddy switched his invention on, and the metal cylinder inside the frame started to rotate. Six and a half seconds later, when the power ran out, the machine whined to a stop and a shower of old plaster was tumbling out of a neatly cut hole halfway up the wall.

'You know, Muddy,' I muttered, 'you really are a genius.'

I blew a layer of dust out of the hole and peered into it. Visible behind the plaster were a couple of thin wooden struts, and tucked behind those, almost out of sight, was something metallic. I scratched at it with my finger, gradually pulling it free, and at last it dropped into the palm of my hand. It was a key, about the same length as my thumb. I held it up for the others to see.

'I don't believe it,' gasped Jack. 'We've been absolutely right, so far.'

'You know what this means, don't you?' giggled

Muddy. 'This must be the key that unlocks the treasure chest! There really is treasure at the end of this!'

I had to admit things were looking good. I stared at the key, wide-eyed, amazed that this little object had been hidden away from the world for so long. For decade after decade, through wars and winters and world events. I felt as if it had been handed to me across the centuries, from Silas Middlewich in 1844 to me, here, now, today.

'Come on, guys,' I said quietly. 'Two more lines to go. We've got work to do.'

CHAPTER
SIX

'WHAT'S THE NEXT LINE?' said Jack.

Mirror the prize and see the trees, fall from the glass and feel the soil.

'Well, the prize must mean the key,' I said.

'Are we supposed to look at it in a mirror?' said Muddy. 'And how would we see a tree if we did?'

I turned the key over and over in my fingers, examining it closely. It was a perfectly ordinary key, without markings or oddities of any kind. It wasn't particularly light or heavy, and it didn't appear to be made of anything unusual.

'It's obviously got some connection to mirroring, or

symmetry, but what?' I mumbled.

'Maths again,' sighed Jack.

'Perhaps it's a reflection, rather than a mirror,' said Muddy. 'The next part of the line mentions glass, and that reflects.'

I snapped my fingers. Which I only did at that moment because I couldn't get a huge exclamation mark to ping into view above my head. 'We're thinking too small. Most of what we've done so far has involved the house itself, and moving around it. We're now standing as far as you can go on *this* side of the house. If we mirror the exact spot we found the key on the *other* side of the house, what do we get?'

As one, we charged out of the room and across the landing at the top of the stairs. Keeping a careful three-dimensional picture in our heads of the key's hiding place, we hurried across the house, judged the correct position as closely as we could and found ourselves at the end of a corridor, standing in front of:

'A side window,' said Jack. '"Mirror the prize and see the trees"!'

'But you can't see any trees from here,' said Muddy, peering out and pulling a face. 'All you can see is the roundabout and the shopping mall.'

'I thought I could hear you lot thundering about.' At

that moment, Izzy appeared along the hallway, clutching a pile of papers to her chest.

'Perfect timing!' I cried. 'Have you found any pictures?'

'Of . . .?'

'Of this house in the 1840s?' I said. 'I need to confirm a theory.'

'Actually, yes,' said Izzy. 'I've been able to find masses of stuff. Here, there're pictures amongst all this.' She handed me the papers and I started flicking through them eagerly.

'Give us the edited highlights of what you've found,' I said, still zipping through one sheet after another. 'This whole mystery contains more questions than two quiz books and a TV game show.'

'OK,' said Izzy, adjusting her specs. 'Tonight's headlines. Silas Middlewich came from a very poor family himself. Which makes the way he exploited poverty-stricken people here all the more shameful, I reckon. He got his money, the money to build this place, by getting involved in buying and selling local plots of land. These deals were highly illegal, it seems. Dozens of wealthy locals, including the mayor, a Mr Carmichael, and a factory owner called Isaac Kenton were also involved, but nothing was ever proved. It's thought that Middlewich got the whole thing hushed up. It's also thought that Middlewich murdered Isaac Kenton's wife. She vanished without trace in 1844, the same year this treasure trail was written. Again, nothing was ever proved.

'And Middlewich was himself murdered?' said Jack.

'Yes, in 1845,' said Izzy. 'By this Martha Humble I mentioned before. Nothing more is known about her, only that she accused him of swindling her husband, whoever he was. Anyway, Middlewich was so hated around town that the local teacher, a man called Josiah Flagg, organised a kind of anti-Middlewich committee. The town constable, Mr Trottman, even had this house raided twice, looking for evidence against Middlewich. But Middlewich was obviously too good at covering his tracks. I tell you, Jack, your parents now own a house built by an absolute and total crook.'

'I'm not so sure,' I muttered to myself. I stopped sorting through Izzy's papers and looked up at the three of them. 'I know who this treasure hunt was meant for. I know who Silas Middlewich meant to leave his treasure to.'

'Who?' said Muddy.

'Think about how the parchment is written, about how we've gone about deciphering it so far. From what Izzy's told us, there was someone who would have had an easier time following this treasure hunt than most people. In 1844, anyway.'

Have you worked out who it was?

'The teacher, Josiah Flagg,' I said. 'Every single clue we've followed has involved exactly the sort of maths, science and history that we learn about even today. Most people in 1844 had no real education at all. Most people would have got hopelessly stuck somewhere along the trail.'

'Noooo,' said Izzy. 'He hated Middlewich. Let's face it, *everyone* hated Middlewich. That *can't* be right.'

'Silas Middlewich left this trail for someone to follow,' I said.

'Even the great Saxby Smart can make one leap of logic too many, you know,' she said, eyeing me with a sly smile.

'You just wait,' I said, eyeing her right back. I turned to the window, brandishing one of the sheets of paper Izzy had brought with her. '*Voilà!*' I declared. 'The trees!'

I showed them what Izzy had printed out at the library. It was an engraving, dated 1860, showing the house from a short distance away. As well as the woods behind the house, there were thickly wooded areas to both sides as well.

'If you'd have looked out of this window in 1844, all you'd have seen would have been trees, trees and more trees. You'd probably still have seen trees in 1944.'

'Right,' said Jack. 'So now . . .'

. . . fall from the glass and feel the soil.

We slid the window open, peeped out and looked directly down. A 'fall from the glass' would have dropped us into the garden. Well, it might have done in 1844. But not any more.

'Oh dear,' said Muddy quietly.

We were looking at the large, plastic roof of a conservatory, added to the side of the house by a more modern owner. Two minutes later, we were looking at that same roof from beneath it. Then we looked down, at the rock-hard floor of concrete under our boots.

Down, and down, and where the saucer goes, go I.

'"Down and down", it says,' wailed Muddy. 'We can't go down through this. Not without some seriously huge equipment.'

'I don't *believe* it!' growled Jack furiously. He stamped against the floor as hard as he could. It was so solid, the blow barely made a sound.

'Isn't there a cellar?' I said.

'Yes, but it's towards the back of the house,' said Jack.

Suddenly, Izzy twitched as if she'd just been jabbed with a stick. 'Wait! Wait!' She quickly searched through her pile of print-outs, tossing sheets aside as she went. 'In amongst that load of documents your parents got with the house, Jack! Plans of the sewers!'

'I am *not* going down a sewer!' cried Jack.

'Of course!' I said. 'That plan would include anything under the house.'

Izzy found the document she was looking for and tapped a finger against it with excitement. 'Look! Look!'

'The cellar goes all the way across here,' I said, tracing the line that marked its edges. 'It extends out past the side of the house, including this spot where we're standing right now. We *can* go down from here.'

Without a moment's hesitation, we raced for the cellar, clattering down a flight of wooden steps into a long, low room lit only by a single bare lightbulb hanging above us. Then we hesitated.

'Urgh, it stinks,' said Izzy.

'It's very damp,' said Jack. 'Dad says it'll be the biggest job in the house, putting it right. It's going to be a boiler room and laundry.'

'We've got to go right over to that far corner,' I said. 'That's the section under the conservatory.'

The cellar was mostly empty. A few decaying wooden crates were stacked to one side, leaning against the moist brickwork of the wall as if they were too exhausted to stand up by themselves. Our boots made dull scraping sounds against the shiny grey flagstoned floor. The single lightbulb beamed claw-like shadows around us as we moved.

Once we were in the right place, we took a good look around.

. . . and where the saucer goes, go I.

'But there's nothing here,' said Jack quietly. His voice sounded thick and heavy, as if the dampness of the walls was soaking it up as he spoke. 'Where on earth would you put a saucer?'

'I assume he means like a china tea-set saucer,' said Muddy. 'Not a flying saucer.'

'I don't think they had aliens in 1844,' said Izzy, pulling a face at the patch of mossy stuff that was growing on the brickwork beside her.

I was also feeling puzzled, to say the least. But the last line had to indicate something down here. I took another close look at everything around me:

1. The ceiling – made up of grey panels that had been nailed in place; obviously not the original ceiling, but a more modern covering of some kind; bashed and gouged in several places.

2. The floor – plain, grey flagstones; almost slippery with damp in places; some of them worn into a dipping, uneven surface, one so deeply you could put your foot in it; with a scattering of dirt and rusted nails.

3. The walls – the same plain brick as the walls in the rest of the house; dark and damp, several of them in a crumbly, flaky state, forming a kind of dotted line at knee height; the mortar between them dotted with black.

'Of course,' I whispered. 'I see it now. It's one of Silas's sideways-thinking clues. All you've got to do is ask yourself, "What does a saucer go under?"'

Can you spot it?

I crouched down and pointed to that deeply worn flagstone in the floor. '"Where the saucer goes, go I." A saucer goes under a cup. That flagstone is worn into . . .'

'Something pretty close to a cup shape,' said Izzy.

'Muddy,' I said, 'got something to get that flagstone up?'

Muddy produced a large screwdriver from his bag and pushed the flat end of it as deep into the crack at the edge of the flagstone as he could. With a few heaves, the stone was lifted. With a loud k-klak it dropped over on its front.

Beneath it, surrounded by earth, was what could only be the lid of a small wooden chest.

'That's it!' cried Jack.

'The treasure!' cried Muddy.

I, being me, didn't want to start sinking my hands into the soil. Eurgh! But Muddy, being Muddy, dived straight in, digging the box free. At last, he hauled it up out of the hole he'd dug and set it down on the shiny floor.

It wasn't very large, but it was very decayed. The wide metal straps that reinforced its edges had become pitted and discoloured over the years. The wood it was made from had been half eaten away by the earth and whatever lived in it.

I took the key we'd found from my pocket and handed

it to Jack. 'It'd probably split open with a good kick,' I said, 'but I think this would be more appropriate.'

With a grin, Jack knelt down and twisted aside the small metal plate that covered the lock. The rest of us hardly dared breathe, our hearts racing. The key turned, and with a crunching sound the lock sprang open.

Jack lifted the lid. Inside, tightly wrapped in a thin sheet of roofing lead to preserve it, was a leather-bound notebook. Every page was filled with handwriting, lists and numbers. Towards the back of it was a torn edge, where a sheet had been ripped out. Inside the front cover, in the same familiar lettering as the parchment, were the words: *Journal of Mr Silas Middlewich, begun 4 June 1837, ended 7 August 1844.*

'That's it?' said Jack. 'That's the treasure of Dead Man's Lane?'

'It certainly is,' I said, smiling broadly. 'It certainly is.'

CHAPTER
SEVEN

IZZY, MUDDY, JACK, JACK'S PARENTS and I assembled in the rubble-strewn tip that was going to be the house's main dining area, once all the refurbishment was complete. It had been a week since we unearthed Silas Middlewich's journal, and I now had the means to put right a great injustice.

The others all sat on upturned packing crates. I stood in front of them holding the journal.

'We expected to find gold and jewels,' I began. 'Or something similar. You're all still asking yourselves: so, what actually happened to Silas Middlewich's ill-gotten gains? Where *did* he hide all the cash he'd squeezed out of those he'd swindled? The answer is: he never had any in the first place.'

'What?' said Izzy. 'That completely contradicts everything that's known about him.'

'Exactly,' I said. 'Everything that's known about him is wrong. This journal proves it. Silas Middlewich had a reputation as a crook and a cruel workhouse owner, but in reality he was the exact reverse. He was a champion of the poor. This house, the workhouse he built, was used to shelter destitute people. He put every penny he had into keeping them safe and properly fed.'

'But how, then, could he get such a terrible reputation?' said Jack.

'Izzy discovered,' I said, 'that he got the money to build this place from various dodgy land deals with local bigwigs. That much is true. I can't say I follow all the legal ins and outs of it, but basically the bigwigs were buying and selling each other's land illegally. They *knew* what they were doing was criminal, but they *thought* Middlewich was on their side. He wasn't. Brilliantly clever of him. He got them paying all kinds of rents and allowances to him, and they couldn't do a thing about it, because every last deal they'd signed would have landed them in jail.'

'So, these landowners then started calling him a crook?' said Jack.

'Exactly,' I said. 'They couldn't go to the police, so they

used their influence to try to ruin Silas Middlewich some other way.'

'Hang on,' said Izzy. 'Surely what Middlewich did was wrong too? I mean, he *did* swindle those landowners, even if he did it for the best of reasons.'

'Absolutely right,' I explained. 'But he realised that these wealthy landowners had a lot more to lose than he did, if it all came out in public. He wasn't interested in his reputation. He didn't care who called him a crook. He'd been born into a poor family, and he saw it as his mission in life to help others in the same position. He was a kind of Victorian Robin Hood!'

'So where does the treasure trail come in?' said Jack's dad, a scattering of plaster dust falling lightly from his hair.

'Ah!' I said, holding up the journal. 'It wasn't long before the landowners were plotting amongst themselves to have Middlewich run out of town. Of course, they wouldn't do their own dirty work, so they persuaded the local schoolteacher to organise efforts against Middlewich.'

'Josiah Flagg,' said Muddy.

'Right,' I said. 'But Middlewich stayed put. Soooo, Plan B, one of the landowners, Isaac Kenton, sends his own wife to Middlewich's workhouse, pretending she's a pauper. The idea is for her to find and destroy any evidence Middlewich has against her husband and his cronies.'

'Good grief,' said Izzy quietly. 'And the landowners spread a rumour that Middlewich had murdered her.'

'Exactly,' I said. 'The perfect way to make Middlewich look like even more of a despicable low-life. The trouble was, Mrs Kenton didn't find the evidence she was looking for. So, somehow, the landowners managed to persuade the police to raid the house twice, and *they* didn't find anything either. Why?'

I paused for a moment. Smiles began to creep across the faces of my audience. Then they began to nod knowingly.

'Because,' I said, 'the evidence was hidden behind that wall panelling. *That* was what the secret compartment was for. Hiding *this* journal. Middlewich was a clever man. He knew those landowners would be after his blood, so he kept every last piece of evidence here, in his journal, safely tucked away, ready for when trouble started brewing.'

'Which it did,' said Jack.

I nodded. 'By now it was 1844. The landowners were up in arms, the police were getting involved, and Middlewich knew that soon the game would be up. He had to pass on his evidence, his journal, his "dark and mighty treasure", to someone who could look after it and take it to the authorities if necessary.'

'Josiah Flagg again,' said Muddy.

'Flagg had secretly been on Middlewich's side all the time,' I said. 'The landowners didn't suspect him. If Middlewich's journal went to Josiah Flagg, it would be safe. The last few days of Middlewich's life are still a mystery, but obviously he felt that his hiding place, behind the panelling, was no longer safe enough. So in the back of his journal he wrote out a treasure trail. He tore out the page, and put the page behind the panelling instead.'

'And it fitted the secret compartment perfectly,' said Izzy, 'because it was torn from the same notebook that the compartment had been designed for in the first place.'

'Yes!' I said. 'He buried the journal in the cellar.'

'And then?' said Muddy.

'And then, the story ends,' I said sadly. 'The journal was buried, and we have nothing to tell us what happened next. My guess is that the undercover Mrs Kenton, and the mysterious Martha Humble, the woman who killed Middlewich, were one and the same.'

'Mrs Kenton murdered him?' said Jack.

'Once we realise that Middlewich wasn't cruel to the

residents of this house, as the official history says, then it doesn't make sense for one of them to have killed him. They'd have no reason to hate him. But Mrs Kenton would. Izzy's research showed us that Middlewich's killer said he'd swindled her husband. Well, we now know what she meant.'

'But why didn't Josiah Flagg get hold of the journal, as Middlewich intended?' said Jack.

I shrugged. 'I guess that's something that will remain a mystery. Perhaps he didn't get the chance to follow the trail. Perhaps the landowners found out about him. Perhaps Middlewich died before he could tell Flagg about the secret compartment. Whatever the truth, time passed, and Silas Middlewich drifted away into history as a crook and a scoundrel. Well, until now. Until Saxby Smart got on the case!'

'But what if it's the journal that's the phoney?' said Izzy. 'What if Middlewich wrote it just to make people change their minds about him?'

'It's a question of character,' I said. 'Remember how I said that the historical accounts of Silas Middlewich didn't match the facts we could deduce about him from the treasure trail? The whole existence of the treasure trail only makes sense once we realise Middlewich was a good guy.'

'You know,' said Jack's dad. 'I bet that journal would be worth something to local historians. Hey, it might even pay for a few tins of paint!'

As it turned out, Jack's dad was right and wrong. Right, because the journal certainly did turn out to be of interest to historians. Wrong, because the sale of the journal at auction a few weeks later didn't pay for a few tins of paint. It paid for the entire refurbishment of the house.

Once everything was sorted out, I returned to my garden shed to write up my notes and sit in my Thinking Chair. The journal is currently on display in a museum. It's strange to think that something that was once so secret is now gawped at every day by visiting parties of school kids. And it's also strange to think that I was able to help a Victorian regain his proper place in history.

Case closed.

CASE FILE SIX:

THE FANGS OF THE DRAGON

CHAPTER ONE

I DON'T KNOW ABOUT YOU, but I always find it odd when I see my teachers out of school. It's as if you don't expect them to have a life beyond the school gates. In your head they're always glugging coffee in the staff room, never filling trolleys at SuperSave.

So I was surprised when, one weekend, Miss Bennett called at my garden shed. She teaches the year group below me and runs the book club I go to once a week after school.

As usual, the *Saxby Smart – Private Detective* sign fell off the door the moment she knocked, and as usual I found myself having to apologise for being unable to nail a simple piece of wood to a door. I slung the sign into a corner, not sure whether to use a bigger nail next time or just to give up having a sign altogether. Paint it! I should paint it on! Of course! Why didn't I think of —

Anyway, I let Miss Bennett sit in my Thinking Chair, and I perched on my desk. It was the middle of summer term, and the assorted gardening stuff I'm forced to share my shed with was giving off the aroma of cut grass. I could feel my hay fever coming on.

Miss Bennett was, as far as I could judge, the youngest teacher in the school. She was certainly one of the most popular. If the descriptive word 'willowy' hadn't already existed, you'd have had to invent it specially for her. She had eyes that looked like they'd been borrowed from a cartoon deer, and a mop of frizzy blond hair that was constantly struggling to free itself from the little hair elastic holding it in a ponytail. She was the last person I'd have expected to present me with one of the oddest cases I've ever come across.

'How can I help you?' I said. I had my arms in a sort of thinking pose, so as to look properly detective-y and on the ball, brain-wise.

'I'm not sure where to begin,' said Miss Bennett. 'I mentioned this problem in the staff room, and several of the other teachers suggested I come and talk to you.'

'I see,' I said. I wasn't sure whether or not it was a good thing to be talked about in the staff room. 'So,

124

what kind of problem is this? Has a crime been committed?'

'Well,' said Miss Bennett, pulling her face into a sort of err-umm-dunno expression, 'more a sort of non-crime, really. In fact, a whole series of non-crimes.'

'You've come to see a private eye about no crime being committed?' I said.

'It's like this,' she explained. 'Six members of my class have had intruders in their homes over the past few weeks.'

'Ah! So each house has been broken into?'

'Nnnnnnno. There's been no sign of forced entry.'

'Ah! So stuff's been stolen?'

'Nnnnnnno. Well, some cash has gone. But there could be other explanations for that.'

'Ah! So burglars have been caught in the act, before they could escape?'

'Nnnnnnno. Nobody's been seen.'

'So,' I said, my eyes narrowing. 'Let's recap. Six members of your class have not had break-ins, have had nothing stolen and have not spotted any shifty-looking blokes in stripy jumpers and eye masks lurking in the bushes. Hmm, yes, I can see they'd be worried.'

'I know it sounds barmy, Saxby, but each of these six is convinced that *someone* has been in their house.'

Now it was my turn to use the err-umm-dunno expression. 'How?'

'That's half the trouble,' said Miss Bennett. 'There's nothing they can be sure about. It's a feeling. They're certain that things have been moved, just slightly. Objects looked at, wardrobes opened, desks picked through. Things like that.'

'Couldn't they just be being, I dunno, oversensitive, or something?'

'I might think that too, but *six* of them? In the same class? Within a few weeks? That seems very odd. And none of them are the sort of kids who'd make things up.'

'Hmm, yes, I see your point. But couldn't it also be a case of one person saying something and the others picking up on it?'

'No,' said Miss Bennett. 'This only came to light because we were having a PSHE lesson the other day. One of the girls, Sarah, happened to mention this peculiar feeling she and her mum had recently experienced, and then the five others spoke up and said they'd experienced exactly the same thing. None of them had mentioned it before, because at the time they all thought, as you would, that it was nothing more than an isolated oddity.'

'You said cash has been taken?' I said.

'Yes, four of these six say that they, or their parents, have missed small amounts of money. A ten-pound note, or some loose change they thought they'd left in a particular place. Again, nothing that's really definite. With no break-ins, nothing else taken, they all thought they'd simply mislaid the money. But now, knowing this has happened six times, the missing money suddenly looks like deliberate theft.'

'It certainly does,' I said. 'But what kind of thief leaves no trace of breaking in, takes nothing but small amounts of cash, and only takes this cash in four instances out of six?'

'Quite,' said Miss Bennett. 'Do you see why I came to you now? My whole class is very worried about this, and so am I. We're all wondering who's going to be next.'

'Haven't any of the six's parents gone to the police?'

'And tell them what?' said Miss Bennett. 'There's still no actual evidence of any crime having been committed at all. What could the police do?'

'Good point,' I said. I hopped up off the desk and on to my feet. 'Well, I can honestly say that's the weirdest problem anyone has ever come to me with. Ever.'

'So . . . you don't think it can be investigated?' said Miss Bennett.

'On the contrary,' I said. I tried to sound confident, but

to be perfectly honest I didn't feel the slightest bit confident at all. This problem seemed totally baffling even before it had begun! However:

'I've never turned down a genuine mystery yet,' I said, 'and I don't intend to start now. Saxby Smart is on the case!'

A Page From My Notebook

Fact: Six households, six no-break-ins, six no-crimes-except-possibly-some-cash-nicked. And yet, firm impressions all round that an intruder had been at work.

Possibility 1: They've all gone a bit barmy. Convenient – all I'd have to do is say 'You've all gone a bit barmy,' and case closed. But not very likely.

Possibility 2: We're dealing with a burglar who walks through walls and doesn't much like stealing things. Not. Very. Likely.

Connection: All these incidents have happened within one small group of people, i.e. one class at school. So! There is a probable link between the incidents and the school. Must investigate further.

Problem: However, this doesn't alter the basic difficulty here, which is that – so far – the only evidence that these incidents took place AT ALL is the gut reactions of those involved!

So! All I've got to go on is feelings. And feelings are not facts. I need facts. Not feelings. Facts. And there are none to go on. Plus, I think my hay fever is really starting to kick in now. I am not happy.

CHAPTER
TWO

WHEN YOU'RE A BRILLIANT SCHOOLBOY detective like me, you can't afford to let anything pass you by. You never know when a clue, or a connection, or a significant fact, will turn up and blow a case wide open. You must always be on the alert. Always.

On Monday morning, I was about as alert as a dead wombat. The pollen count was at an all-time high, and my nose was at an all-time low. I slouched to school, cursing the DNA of my parents for passing on the hay fever gene to their only child! I couldn't decide which were runnier, my eyes or my nostrils. I was not in the best of condition to observe and deduce.

Even so, taking my usual route across the park at 8.40 a.m., I noticed something very odd. If you've read my previous volume of case files, you'll be well aware of that low-down rat Harry Lovecraft. He's in my class at school but, as I like to say, the rest of us out-class him in every way, ha ha. Harry Lovecraft is my arch enemy, a sneaky, smarmy, shiny-haired and shiny-shoed weasel, who's about as trustworthy as a starving cobra in a boxful of white mice. If there's a con trick to be played in the playground, he'll play it.

So I was naturally suspicious when I saw him, taking his usual route across the park, chatting amiably to a group of younger kids. Believe me, that low-down rat Harry Lovecraft never chats amiably to anyone, least of all kids in the year groups below him. Tricks them out of their dinner money, yes, but chats amiably, no.

I walked faster and caught up with the group. They seemed to be talking about wizards, frog-people, and something called a 'Grand Croak Toad Belcher'.

'What are you ubb to, Lovecraft?' I said.

'Deary me, Smart,' oozed Harry Lovecraft, 'is that hay fever, or has someone finally given you the smack in the face you deserve?'

The kids around him giggled. Some of them were from Miss Bennett's class, and the rest from the other class in that year group.

I tried to think of a witty reply. I couldn't. 'Just shudd

131

ubb, Lovecraft,' I said. 'You're ubb to something.'

'We're talking about FrogWar BattleZone,' piped up one of the kids. 'You collect the figures and paint them. We're all making our own battleboards.'

I glared at Harry Lovecraft as best I could with my bloodshot, pollen-bloated eyes. 'You're never into FrogWar,' I said. 'Whadd sneaky liddle plot are you haddching now?'

Harry Lovecraft took a step closer to me. A new Inkspot pen, one of the more expensive sort, gleamed in the top pocket of his school uniform. Clipped to his lapel was the latest miniature MP3 player, a model that had only been in the shops for a week or so.

'That's the trouble with busybodies like you, Smart,' he sneered, 'you always think the worst of people.'

'No, not peeble in general,' I sneered back. 'Just you.'

I turned to leave. Or rather, to carry on walking ahead of them. I'd only gone a few steps when I turned back, with a question for Harry.

'Your birthday's not for three muddths yet, is it?' I said.

'What?' blinked Harry, confused. 'Planning a surprise party for me, are you?'

I walked on. Despite having a fit of sneezing that lasted all the way to school, I was secretly congratulating myself. I now had *two* reasons for thinking that Harry Lovecraft might somehow be involved in these mysterious non-break-ins I was investigating, two coincidences which made me suspicious.

Have you spotted them?

The two coincidences were:

1. Harry Lovecraft's little FrogWar group included a number of Miss Bennett's pupils. He would *never* normally be friendly with those kids. Was there a link between his sudden interest, and the non-break-ins experienced by Miss Bennett's class?

2. Some money had – probably, apparently – gone missing. And Harry Lovecraft suddenly owned an expensive pen and an MP3 player he couldn't have bought before it arrived in the shops last week. From past experience I knew he was enough of a low-down rat to resort to petty theft.

The problem was, *how* could Harry Lovecraft be linked with these 'un-crimes'? As far as I knew, he hadn't suddenly gained the ability to walk through walls, as this phantom-like burglar appeared to be doing.

On the *plus* side: these un-crimes clearly showed a great deal of careful sneakiness – classic Lovecraft trademarks!

But! On the *minus* side: to be so careful and sneaky seemed a bit of a wasted effort, if all that was nicked was some cash. If Harry Lovecraft wanted cash, he generally just pulled another dinner-money scam.

But! On the *plus* side: no news of another dinner-money scam had reached me this term. So Harry Lovecraft's sudden flaunting of new goodies made a link with the un-crimes all the more likely.

But! On the *minus* side: would even that low-down rat turn to actual burglary? I'd never known him go *that* far, ever.

By the time I arrived at school, not only was my nose bunged up with snot, but my brain was bunged up with a jumble of confusing and contradictory thoughts. Before registration, I hurried along to Miss Bennett's class and arranged for the six victims of the un-crimes to stay behind at morning break. I had three items on my To Do list:

- Talk to these six, and find out more about each individual incident.
- Keep a close eye on H Lovecraft.
- Get hold of some more tissues. The ones I'd brought from home were already reduced to damp shreds.

While our form teacher, Mrs Penzler, was handing out worksheets for the first lesson of the day, I leaned across to the desk beside me and had a quiet word with my friend George 'Muddy' Whitehouse, as follows:

Me: (checking that neither Mrs Penzler nor H Lovecraft were looking my way) Muddy, I'm going to be busy on a case during break. Can you keep a close watch on Harry Lovecraft for me?

Muddy: Will do. Brilliant. I've got some of my home-made spy gear with me.

Me: Why do you have to keep bringing spies into everything?

Muddy: Spies are cool.

Me: So are fridges, so what? We are not spies. This is detective work.

Muddy: (pulling a face) . . . It's similar to spies.

Me: No, it's not, it's — (flapping hands about) Just forget about spies. Watch Harry Lovecraft. Don't let him know you're keeping tabs on him, OK? Be casual. Be subtle.

Muddy: Casual and subtle, check. (Pause) 'The seagulls fly south over Moscow.'

Me: . . . What?

Muddy: It's what spies say.

Me: Oh shut up.

Mrs Penzler: Saxby, less chatter, please!

Me: Sorry!

The moment the bell for morning break sounded, I zipped along to Miss Bennett's class. I talked to each of the six one by one, and made careful notes. Here are the results.

Incident 1
Pupil's name: Maggie Hamilton
Date/time/location of incident: 24 April (first Thursday of term)/between 10 a.m. and 1 p.m./14 Meadow Road

What happened: Maggie's mum came home, thought several things had been moved – computer keyboard, address book by kitchen phone, pile of household bills; £20 note in hall drawer gone. Mum has large jewellery box in bedroom – untouched.

Any other relevant info: Mum and Dad think Mum's just mistaken (neighbour says she saw Mum arriving home at 11.30 a.m., Mum thought she didn't get back until 1 p.m.); Dad was away on business all that week; Mum works afternoons at SuperSave.

Incident 2

Pupil's name: Patrick Atwood

Date/time/location of incident: 1 May/in the morning 'sometime after 10.15 a.m.'/26 Avon Street

What happened: Files and papers on desk disturbed; drawers sorted through.

Any other relevant info: Patrick's mum works from home – this happened on the only day of the week she's not at home; very worried that 'intruder' knew this and/or was watching the house.

Incident 3

Pupil's name: Sarah Hardy (This was the pupil who first mentioned the 'un-crimes' in class)

Date/time/location of incident: 8 May/'must have been between 9.45 a.m. and noon' / Flat 2, Park Court

What happened: Stuff around PC station moved; waste paper basket in living room 'in wrong position'; pile of change on hall shelf gone; £10 note from Mum's dressing table gone (credit cards untouched).

Any other relevant info: Mum thinks Sarah's two older sisters swiped the money; sisters grounded; sisters *not* happy; only Sarah noticed item movements – sisters distracted by college work, Mum distracted by daily hobby of shopping(!); Mum calls Sarah's suggestion of an intruder 'ridiculous'.

Incident 4

Pupil's name: Thomas Waters

Date/time/location of incident: 15 May/'sometime late morning'/36 Field Close

What happened: Drawers left slightly open; box of old paperwork disturbed; kitchen bin moved; £20 in assorted coins and notes gone from teapot in kitchen(!?), but Mum has convinced herself she used this for Chinese takeaway the previous week.

Any other relevant info: Thomas's mum suspicious when returned home from appointment; Thomas's dad always at work 7 a.m.–7 p.m.; Mum works with Maggie

Hamilton's mum at SuperSave in the afternoons, and is friends with Liz Wyndham's mum down the street.

Incident 5

Pupil's name: Liz Wyndham

Date/time/location of incident: 22 May/before 12 p.m./45 Field Close

What happened: Work desk disturbed; computer screen angle changed; wardrobes gone through.

Any other relevant info: Liz's mum works from home part-time – only leaves house a couple of times a week due to medical stuff. Liz asked nosy Mrs Huxley from across the street if she'd seen anything that day ('she misses *nothing*') – Mrs H claimed Liz's mum left house at 9.20 a.m., came back at 10.50 a.m., left again at 11.05 a.m. and returned again at 12! But Liz's mum says she was out all morning, from 9.20. Liz worried about her mum!

Incident 6

Pupil's name: John Wurtzel

Date/time/location of incident: 29 May/'had to be 10.15– 11.45 a.m'/177 Deadman Lane

What happened: Cupboard in dining room opened; laptop lid down when had been up; bills pinned to corkboard moved slightly; glass bowl on mantelpiece emptied of loose change.

Any other relevant info: John's parents are divorced – Dad is an office manager, Mum is an artist — she spends most of every day in her studio in the attic. Mum thinks Dad turned up and moved stuff around just to confuse and annoy her(!)

Looking through these notes on the way back to class, *lots* of interesting links and possibilities leaped out at me faster than a pouncing tiger. Links involving dates, times, even the nature of the incidents themselves.

I could see three remarkable coincidences, one really weird connection, and – argh! – something which more or less proved Harry Lovecraft could *not* be the intruder. How many of your conclusions agree with mine?

ITEM 1 – three remarkable coincidences:

1. The timing of each incident. In every case, it happened on a *Thursday* (the dates are seven days apart)! And on a Thursday *morning* too, between about a quarter to ten and one o' clock!

2. The households involved. In every case, there was *no dad* around at the time of the incident – every dad was either at work, or away, or absent for one reason or another. *And*, leading on from that: it struck me as very odd that all these six mums were people who just happened to be free on those Thursday mornings. They worked for themselves, or they worked in the afternoons, or whatever. They were all people who, on those Thursday mornings, could organise their own timetable.

3. The stuff that was disturbed. Strangely similar in each case – household papers, stuff in drawers, and computers in particular. That simply *had* to be significant!

ITEM 2 – one really weird connection:

In two cases out of the six, the relevant mum was seen by somebody to be at home at a time when she claimed to be out. Maggie Hamilton's mum and Liz Wyndham's mum were both spotted by neighbours.

Now, if that had happened in *one* case, I'd have put it down to a simple mistake. Someone got their times wrong. But it happened *twice*, and it happened twice within this very specific, already coincidence-packed group of six. Now *that's* weird!

ITEM 3 – Harry Lovecraft now had a perfect alibi: Thursday mornings, he was at school.

Hmm . . .

On my way back to class, my hay fever a bit better now that I'd been away from fresh air for a while, I got a full report from Muddy on what that low-down rat Harry Lovecraft had been up to during break. The report was pretty much exactly what I was expecting.

'He's been talking to various kids in the year below us,' whispered Muddy, as everyone filed back into the classroom, 'and several in the year below that as well.'

'Good work,' I whispered.

'There was a lot of chit-chat about giant frogs, or something, I didn't really follow that bit. But I think that was just a cover. What he was trying to find out was personal details. What their parents do for a living, what area their house is in, that kind of thing.'

'Excellent work,' I whispered. 'I suppose these kids didn't suspect him of anything?'

'No,' whispered Muddy. 'They think they've got some

great new mate. He keeps claiming he can get a discount on these frog-whatsernames.'

'Brilliant work,' I whispered. 'How did you get all this information? Careful listening and deduction?'

'No, I went up to them and asked.'

'You *what*?' I cried. Several of our classmates turned in our direction. 'I told you to be casual and subtle!'

'You told me not to use my spy gear!' protested Muddy. 'I had the *Whitehouse Listen-O-Phone 2000* with me in my bag, but oooh nooo, not allowed. I haven't got super-powered hearing, you know! I can't eavesdrop from the other end of the playground!'

'Harry's going to know we're investigating him now,' I hissed.

'Tut tut,' said a voice behind us, a voice that was slimier than a snail's handshake. That low-down rat Harry Lovecraft swanned past us, grinning his sickly grin. 'Tut tut, Smart; is one of your trained poodles not doing its tricks correctly?'

Muddy made a remark about tricks and trained poodles that can't be repeated in these pages. From the other side of the classroom, Mrs Penzler clacked a ruler on her desk for attention.

'Is there a problem? Saxby Smart? George Whitehouse?'

'Sorry!' I cried.

A Page From My Notebook

Further important thoughts arising from the Harry Lovecraft connection, and from my investigations so far:

Obviously, nobody's walking through walls. The intruder is either using actual keys to get in, or is a superb lock-picker. As yet, there are no leads whatsoever on this point. The intruder has clearly made quite an effort to gain entry, and yet has taken very little. WHY? It must have something to do with the items that were disturbed.

Vital Question: What is this intruder really looking for? And WHAT is going on with those two mums who were seen at home when they said they weren't at home? To have the INTRUDER seen at those times would make sense, but those neighbours positively identified the mums, NOT a stranger.

Conclusion: Huh???

IMPORTANT POINT: I have no reason to suppose that the intruder is going to stop at six break-ins. Who's going to be next?

All this leads to a specific question: I need to know exactly what the six mums were doing while they were out on each 'incident' day!

CHAPTER THREE

BEFORE THE END OF THE SCHOOL DAY, I asked the six affected pupils in Miss Bennett's class the specific question that my notes had suggested. The following morning, I had six specific answers.

Maggie Hamilton: 'She left at ten, drove to the Post Office, then she was at something called Monsieur Jacques's De-Stress Session from half ten to half eleven. Then she drove into town for lunch with my gran, then home at one o'clock.'

Patrick Atwood: 'At quarter past ten she walked to her weekly de-stress session, which is run by some French bloke from Dragonfang Gym. Then after that she did some shopping at SuperSave, then came home.'

Sarah Hardy: 'After leaving home she popped into the

dentist's to make an appointment, then she was at Monsieur Jacques's class until half eleven, then straight back.'

Thomas Waters: 'She says the only place she went was to her regular de-stress class. I said to her "De-stress? Distress, more like," because she's so wound-up you'd think she was clockwork. And she said to me "Stop being a cheeky little so-and-so and lay the table". . .' etc., etc.

Liz Wyndham: 'Mum went to the doctor's for 9.45. After that, she went to a weekly thing Dragonfang Gym organise. Then back home at midday.'

John Wurtzel: 'She's got it all in her diary, apparently. Quarter past ten, leaves the house to go to her stress-free meeting, or something like that. Then back home and she was in her studio the rest of the day.'

'Bingo,' I said quietly to myself, smiling a huge smile. Then I stopped smiling and said 'Uh-oh!', not at all quietly.

Today was Tuesday. On Thursday there would be another of this Monsieur Jacques's classes. During which, someone, somewhere, was going to get a visit . . .

I had two days to track down the intruder!

Think, think, think! Find out whose mums would be attending Thursday's class. That would give me all the addresses where the intruder might strike next. But how could I know which address would be next on the intruder's list?

There was only one way to proceed: to get as much info as possible on this Monsieur Jacques and Dragonfang Gym. In the main hall at lunchtime, while everyone was chewing on cardboard-like pie crust and trying to hide their uneaten peas from the dinner ladies, I talked to my friend Izzy. As those who've examined my earlier case files will know, Isobel Moustique is St Egbert's number one classroom genius, and quite possibly the girliest girl on the face of the earth. I told her the story so far as I struggled to cut into my piece of pie.

'So,' I said, gritting my teeth as I leaned as heavily as I dared on my knife and fork, 'I need all the background info you can give me on both the gym and the French guy.'

'No problem,' she said. 'This Monsieur Jacques person has only been in the health and fitness business a few months, but he's already built up quite a large list of clients. He holds all his classes in people's homes – yoga, weight training, relaxation, the usual thing. Each member of the class takes it in turn to host a session. He's not been going very long, as I said, but he's already planning to close Dragonfang Gym at the end of the year.

Apparently, he and his wife are moving to Africa to do charity work.'

'You're amazing,' I gasped, open-mouthed. 'I simply name a subject, and you know all about it! Incredible!'

'Nnnnot really,' said Izzy, pulling a you-poor-dumb-fool face. 'My mum's just signed up for one of their classes.'

'Ah,' I said quickly, 'yes, I thought so, of course.' I shovelled some peas on to my fork. They fell off.

'And before you ask,' said Izzy, 'no, my mum's class is not on a Thursday morning. It's tonight, at six.'

'That's perfect,' I said. 'Could she get me in there? I want to observe this Monsieur Jacques at close hand.'

'I don't think they normally have kids at these sessions,' said Izzy, 'but I'm sure we can think of something.'

I chewed my way through a particularly tough section of pastry. 'Aren't you having the pie?' I said.

She gave my plate one of her arch, feline looks. 'As if,' she said. She unzipped her pink sandwich bag and took out a pot of home-made pasta salad and a fork.

CHAPTER
FOUR

HAVE YOU EVER NOTICED HOW the members of some families seem almost identical, while the members of other families seem about as alike as a pot of jam and the Empire State Building?

Izzy's mum was as unlike her daughter as it was possible for two people to be, without major genetic re-sequencing. Whereas Isobel was all glitzy trousers and chunky rings, her mother was sombre and businesslike.

At six o'clock that evening, as we stood together on the doorstep of number 29, Mercia Way, Izzy's mum looked ready to march into a high-powered, top-level executive meeting and start firing people. And that's not an easy look to achieve in a tracksuit. I still had my school uniform on.

149

The door was opened by the owner of the house, Mrs Ferguson. It was her turn to host this week's session.

'Hallo, hallo,' she twittered, ushering us inside. 'Lovely to see you, Caroline. Who's this with you?'

I'd given Izzy's mum my carefully thought-out cover story. I was to be Matt, her adopted nephew. I was to be staying with her while my house was repaired following a gas explosion. I was to be accompanying her this evening due to the traumatic after-effects of having my house blown up.

'This,' said Izzy's mum, 'is my daughter's friend Saxby. He's just tagging along.'

'Nice to meet you,' said Mrs Ferguson. 'The more the merrier; do come along in, Monsieur Jacques has arrived and we're ready to start.'

As we walked to the living room, I nudged Izzy's mum in the ribs.

'What about my carefully thought-out cover story?' I whispered.

'Don't be silly,' said Izzy's mum. 'Half the people here will know you from school. What on earth do you need a cover story for?'

'It's more detective-y,' I grumbled.

Assembled in the living room were a dozen other women in tracksuits. Standing in front of them was a man with a hairdo shaped like a headless duck, and a moustache that set a whole new standard for the phrase 'thin and weedy'. He wore bright yellow trousers, and a polo-neck pullover with *Dragonfang* printed across the chest. A gold badge with a dragon logo on it was pinned above the lettering.

So this was Monsieur Jacques. Immediately, his face seemed vaguely familiar to me.

'Good evening, everyone,' he cried, clapping politely for quiet. (For the full effect here, you need to read his words in a French accent as thick as week-old gravy.) 'To business! *Voilà!* We 'ave ze beginning exercise! Aaaaand . . .'

Everyone lined up and started sticking their legs out at weird angles. I nudged Izzy's mum again.

'I forgot to ask,' I whispered. 'Which class is this, exactly? Advanced Relaxation? Meditation For Beginners?'

'Ballet-robics,' said Izzy's mum. 'Come on, get those arms moving.'

Thumpy music started up on the CD player. If my heart had sunk any lower, I'd have been standing on it. 'Great,' I muttered to myself.

I reminded myself that I was here to make careful observations. I was troubled by the fact that Monsieur

Jacques seemed strangely familiar. And I was even more troubled by his accent. Something, as Monsieur Jacques would probably say, smelled of ze fish.

'That's it, *mes amis*!' cried Monsieur Jacques. 'Kick and twirl! And one, two, three, one, two, three! That is good, Mrs Ferguson! Also good, Mrs Moustique!'

After a few minutes, he shut up a bit and started patrolling each of his pupils, tapping out the rhythm of the music with his fingers. I took the chance to ask him some deceptively innocent questions. The first of these questions was based on a snippet of historical knowledge I'd learned during the case of *The Treasure of Dead Man's Lane* . . .

'This is a really brilliant class, Monsieur Jacques,' I said, above the music's beat. 'Absolutely outstanding.'

He glanced at me as if I was something he'd recently picked from his nose. '*Merci*,' he said. 'Aaaand one, two —'

'Why did you call your gym Dragonfang?' I said. 'Why not something more French; maybe something historical like "Waterloo". You know, to commemorate Napoleon's victory?'

He tapped at his gold dragon badge. 'Yes, of course I considered "Waterloo", but I am ze, as you say, fan of ze martial arts movies. My favourite, it eez *Dragon Warrior*

Goes Nuts in Shanghai. You know it?'

'*Oui!* Or, as it translates into French, *Le Penzler de Bennett Izzy de la Muddi*, yeh?'

'*Oui*, exactly,' he said. 'Now then, come along, one, two —'

'But I hear you're closing the gym soon?' I said, putting on my best sorrowful-puppy-dog expression.

'Yes,' said Monsieur Jacques, 'ze Mrs wife and I, we do ze work for ze charity in Africa; we 'elp orphans build ze shelters for endangered species in ze Brazilian rainforest. Soon we sell up and move there.' He clapped his hands and raised his voice. 'In time with ze music! Good! Lovely work, everyone! Three, four, five . . .'

I knew it! The guy was a total phoney, no more French than my Auntie Pat. And I doubted he could even point to Africa on a map showing nothing but Africa, with Africa marked in red, and a sign saying *Africa, This Way* printed on it!

Did you spot his three mistakes?

1. Napoleon LOST the Battle of Waterloo. (For more info, see my previous case file.)

2. That translation I gave him was total gibberish. Even I speak more French than him, and all I can manage is to order a baguette!

3. The Brazilian rainforest is in South America. In, like, you know, er, *Brazil*! It's nowhere near Africa.

I tapped at Monsieur Jacques's sleeve. 'Could I ask if you —?'

He was clearly getting ever so slightly fed up with my questions now. 'I don't appear to 'ave your name on my list, young man. 'Ave you paid for ze session?'

'Er, no, I'm just tagging along,' I said.

'Well, tag along to ze kitchen and make ze tea,' said Monsieur Jacques. He gave me a smarmy smile.

And in that instant, I knew why his face had looked familiar. Remember what I said about family resemblances? Monsieur Jacques's smarmy smile was identical to the smarmy smile of a certain low-down rat from school . . .

My heart suddenly started to race. So as not to give anything away to 'Monsieur Jacques', I quickly retreated to the kitchen. While the kettle boiled, I phoned Izzy.

'Stand by,' I said. 'I'll get a picture of him and send it to you straight away.'

'Okey-dokey,' she said.

I hurried back into the living room, holding the phone to my ear as if Izzy was still on the line. I planned to stand as close to our phoney French friend as I could, pretend to be deep in conversation, and click the photo button when he wasn't looking.

The living room was empty.

For a second or two I panicked, thinking that the class was suddenly over and that everyone had gone home. But as the steady throb of the music continued, I could hear people moving about all over the house.

One or two members of the class reappeared, and kick-stepped their way across the room. I spotted a couple more of them twirling and stretching in the hallway. From somewhere upstairs came a familiar, treacle-thick accent: 'Looovely, Mrs Ferguson, hold your leg in zat position and spin! Yeeees, that is perfecto; you three there, please to be going downstairs to join ze group in ze dining room. Loooovely!'

I found Izzy's mum doing funny-looking arm movements on the stairs.

'Does every class include this different-rooms routine?' I asked.

'Oh yes,' said Izzy's mum, continuing to wave her arms about like a slow-motion windmill, 'we always split up, spread out and move about. Monsieur Jacques says it's to give us a free-flowing feeling of personal space. He says it allows him to assess us individually.'

A crime-related thought popped into my mind. 'Yes,' I said, 'and I bet that's not all it allows him to do.'

Monsieur Jacques appeared at the top of the stairs and started skipping lightly down towards us. 'Mrs Ferguson,' he called back over his shoulder, 'ze spinning, she is enough now, you will get dizzy again.'

As he drew level with Izzy's mum and me, he smiled at one of us and sneered at the other. I'll leave you to guess which of us got the sneer.

'You 'ave made ze tea?' he said.

'*Oui*,' I replied. 'Ze kettle, she is boiled.'

For the briefest of split seconds, the look on his face said, 'I don't like you, sunshine!' But then he switched his attention to Izzy's mum, grinning soppily at her. He dug into his pocket and produced a gold badge like the one he was wearing, with a dragon logo printed on it.

'Mrs Moustique!' he declared. 'You 'ave made such terrific effort this evening. You are quite a new member to our group, but already I award you my Star Pupil badge!'

'Oh, thank you very much,' said Izzy's mum, as he pinned it to her tracksuit. There was a ripple of applause from upstairs.

I took the opportunity, while Monsieur Jacques's

attention was diverted, to flip open my phone. I got an excellent shot of his face while he was busy asking Izzy's mum for her monthly subscription fee.

Later, after I'd sent the picture to Izzy and was back home, I waited nervously for confirmation of the evening's findings. I didn't have to wait very long. Izzy called me back within the hour.

'You were right to suggest I look back through crime reports on the news sites,' she said. 'It didn't take me long to find this Monsieur Jacques. The pictures I've got of him are ten years old, but it's definitely the same guy.'

'Ten years old?' I said. 'Why's that?'

'Because until the middle of last year, he was in prison,' said Izzy. 'He organised a gang that conned half a million quid out of a group of Third World aid charities. What a scumbag!'

'And his real name?'

'Oh yeh, that's the best bit,' said Izzy. 'You were quite right. He certainly isn't French. He's Harry's uncle. His name is Jack Lovecraft.'

That piece of information was the last piece in the puzzle. I now knew exactly what had been going on. I knew what those non-break-ins were all about, and I knew what Harry had been up to.

But catching the intruder would still be difficult.

CHAPTER FIVE

THURSDAY 10.55 A.M.

'Can't we park outside the house?' asked Miss Bennett.

'No!' I cried. 'We mustn't be seen, we can't let the intruder suspect anything.'

Miss Bennett stopped the school minibus and we all got out: Miss Bennett, me, the six pupils in Miss Bennett's class who'd already been visited by the intruder and a seventh pupil, a scruffy boy called Oliver.

'I live at the other end of this street,' said Oliver, as Miss Bennett locked up the minibus.

'Exactly,' I said. 'That's why we're here. OK, everyone, most of these houses have hedges around their front gardens. Keep down, below the hedges, out of sight.'

Everyone crouched down and shuffled along the street towards Oliver's house. An old lady walking a tiny dog passed us on the other side of the road. Both of them gave us a funny look.

'Honestly, Saxby,' said Miss Bennett crossly, 'is this really necessary?'

'It's vital,' I whispered.

'Why couldn't you have talked to us at school?' said Miss Bennett.

'Because until we've caught the intruder red-handed, news mustn't get out at school that the mystery's been solved. One sneaky phone call from Harry Lovecraft, and the intruder will fold up the whole scheme and make a run for it. I've got Muddy covering for me back in class. As far as Harry's concerned, I'm at the optician's getting my glasses adjusted.'

'You're making some pretty serious allegations about that boy,' said Miss Bennett quietly. 'You'd better have your facts straight.'

By now, we'd reached Oliver's house. Luckily, the hedge round his garden was particularly tall and thick. We all scrunched down, at a point where we couldn't be seen from the front door or any of the windows.

I checked my watch. 11 a.m. precisely.

'OK,' I said. 'Now, we all know that, right at this

moment, there's a weekly de-stress session going on, which the mums of all seven of you are attending. This week, it's over at Liz Wyndham's house.'

'Right,' said Liz Wyndham.

'The homes of six members of that class have already been visited by a mysterious intruder,' I said. 'Oliver here is the only person we know of whose mum is at that class, but whose home has *not* yet been visited by a mysterious intruder.'

'Wait a moment,' said Miss Bennett. 'Surely, there are more than seven people at this weekly session? How can we know which house is next on the intruder's list?'

'Weeeeeell,' I said, 'strictly speaking, we can't . . .'

'So, we could all be crouching here, behind a hedge, like a bunch of idiots, using up lesson time, for nothing?' said Miss Bennett.

'Strictly speaking . . . yes,' I admitted. 'But I have every reason to believe I'm right, and that the intruder is, right now, as we speak, in Oliver's house.'

'Well, let's get in there and grab them, then!' cried Oliver.

'Shhh!' I hissed. 'No good. If we barge in there, the intruder could simply dump the evidence we need and run out of the back door. We have to wait. We have to catch them.'

'But what's this evidence you mention?' said Miss Bennett. 'And how *do* you know this is the right house?'

'Look at what we know so far,' I said. 'In every case, the intruder has struck at a house they *know* will be empty. Think about it from the intruder's point of view. Mum X attends a gym class. So *she's* out of the house, but half a dozen *more* people might still be at home! An intruder will want to minimise the risk of finding the place still occupied. *That* is the link between all seven of you here. All seven of you can confirm to a third party that, on a Thursday morning, when Mum's at her gym class, there's nobody else at home.'

'A third party?' said Oliver.

'You mean . . . Harry Lovecraft?' said Miss Bennett.

'Exactly!' I said. 'He's been unusually friendly of late. He's been chatting away to people left, right and centre. And the interest he takes in all his new friends covers up the fact that he's fishing for information. About your mums and dads, about what goes on at home . . .'

'That sneaky, miserable, underhand . . .' muttered Liz Wyndham.

'So,' said Miss Bennett, 'cross-referencing the addresses of the people who attend the gym class, with the information gathered by Harry, means that the intruder can know which houses would make the best targets.'

'Exactly,' I said. 'Of course, the intruder only *needs* to have an address, and can use various tricks to find out if there's someone else at home, but the information provided by Harry would be a perfect shortcut to targeting houses left unattended.'

'But we're still no nearer knowing *how* or *why* these incidents are happening,' said Miss Bennett. 'The intruder can't be the man running the classes. He's running the classes.'

'How is Monsieur Jacques involved?' said Liz Wyndham. 'My mum thinks the world of him.'

'I'm afraid Monsieur Jacques is really Monsieur Harry Lovecraft's uncle, a man with a criminal record as long as an anteater's tongue. He got out of prison last year, set up Dragonfang Gym and is using it as a front for his latest con trick.'

'You mean he's holding all these classes as a kind of distraction, so that the intruder can get to work?' said Miss Bennett.

'Oh, he's doing a lot more than that,' I said. 'Remember how there's never any sign of an actual break-in? That's because the intruder is using a key. You see, because Monsieur Jacques holds his classes in people's homes, he's got every opportunity to snoop. He sends people off around the house, doing their exercises, and all he needs is a few seconds to locate the owner's keyring, and take an impression of their keys with a bar of soap or a block of modelling clay.'

'But if he's going to all that trouble,' said Miss Bennett. 'Why is so little being taken?'

'On the contrary,' I said. 'A great deal is being taken. Look at the sort of things that were disturbed in each case. Computers, household papers, even waste paper bins. The intruder is stealing words and numbers.'

'Words and numbers?' said Oliver.

'Bank account numbers, computer passwords, login details, financial records. Personal information of all kinds. Identity theft.'

'But none of the parents have had their bank accounts emptied, or anything like that,' said Miss Bennett. 'Surely he's not simply storing up all that information?'

'Yes, that's precisely what he's doing,' I said. 'He's already told everyone he's closing Dragonfang Gym down and moving abroad. Not to Africa, as he claims, I'm sure. But somewhere. And when he's safely on the other side of the world, he can use all that information to whatever criminal ends he likes. It's all done by computer. He could be on Mars and still launch raids on one bank account after another.'

'Of course,' said Miss Bennett, 'if he's abroad, it'll be

that much harder to trace him, and that much harder for the law to catch up with him.'

'Quite,' I said. 'He's been running loads of different classes, so by now he's probably got passwords and account numbers for dozens of people, possibly hundreds.'

'If that's true,' said Liz Wyndham, 'why haven't more people in more gym classes noticed that these intrusions are happening?'

'Why would they? You lot only noticed by accident. If the intruder is careful enough, most of this scheme's victims won't even realise the intruder's visited them.'

'Why steal the money?' said Liz Wyndham. 'Isn't that inviting suspicion?'

'A little bonus for Harry?' I said. 'For services rendered? If Harry wasn't so flash with his cash, I might not have noticed that! In most cases, for most classes, Monsieur Jacques will have had to spend time cosying up to his customers to find out the sort of household details that the intruder would benefit from. But once he realised that several members of this one particular Thursday morning de-stress class were mums at St Egbert's, he spotted an opportunity. He had a nephew he could use as an inside man!'

'So *who* is in my house, then?' wailed Oliver. 'Who *is* this intruder?'

I was about to answer him when two things happened. First, the front door of Oliver's house swung open. Second, I felt a distinct and sudden itching in my nose. I glanced at the hedge: it was one of those flowering types. I'd been crouching down with my head in an air current loaded with pollen.

'Ohhh, briddiant!' I sighed.

But I had no time to feel sorry for myself. The door of Oliver's house was standing ajar. So far, no movement came from inside.

Nobody dared breathe. We all stared through the tiny gaps in the hedge, between the leaves, watching the front door.

11.04 a.m.

Suddenly, moving swiftly, a figure emerged. A woman. She was wearing a long red coat and chunky boots, and a cascade of blond hair fell around her shoulders. She was facing into the house, away from us, as if checking that she'd not forgotten anything. The upper part of her was deep in the slab of shadow thrown by the flat porch that jutted out above the door.

'Nobobby bake a sound,' I whispered. 'She bite rubb away before we cabb get her.'

'Who is she?' whispered Miss Bennett.

Oliver made a slight whimpering noise. 'I don't believe it. That's my mum. My mum is the intruder.'

The woman shut the front door behind her with a clunk. She took a key from the pocket of her coat and double-locked the door, giving it a rattle to make sure it was firmly closed.

'So your mum's been the intruder all along?' gasped Liz Wyndham.

'Hang on a minute,' whispered Oliver. 'This is her own house . . .'

'Be quiedd,' I breathed. 'She muddn't . . . know . . . we're . . . AHHHH-CHOOOO!' My sneeze was so loud it sent a flock of sparrows into a panic at the other end of the street.

Instantly, the woman spun round. Spooked, she made a dash for the gate at the side of the house.

We all leaped from our hiding place. Miss Bennett, with that willowy frame of hers, would have made a good athlete. She caught up with the woman in less than a dozen loping strides, grabbing her by the shoulders.

The woman cried out angrily. As she tried to wriggle free of Miss Bennett's grip, she overbalanced and toppled on to the front lawn.

As she did so, her long blond hair came loose. The

wig dropped to the grass, revealing a short, dark haircut underneath.

'Good grief!' cried Oliver, from the back of the group. 'My mum wears a . . . Hey!'

'I thingg you'll find your bubb is safely at her gybb class,' I said, borrowing a hanky from Liz Wyndham. 'Say hallo to Uncle Jack's wife, Harry Lovecraft's Auntie Sharon.'

Miss Bennett had her securely pinned down on the grass. Auntie Sharon glared up at us, a mixture of anger and defiance on her face.

'But why was she disguised as my mum?' said Oliver. 'How does she even know what my mum looks like?'

I blew my nose a couple of times. 'I told you Harry's uncle, Monsieur Jacques, had been busy snooping around all your houses whenever he held a class there,' I said. 'As well as copying keys, he also looked in wardrobes. His wife here, the intruder, could then get hold of similar clothes and hair, and disguise herself as the correct mum every time. With the right key, and the right look, anybody who saw her come and go would think they were seeing someone else. Which happened twice, remember. Those nosy neighbours didn't see your mums, they saw Auntie Sharon here.'

With Auntie Sharon pinned on her side, items were

starting to drop out of the pockets of her coat. The house key she'd used, a pair of gloves and a jotter pad. I stooped down and picked the jotter pad up. Clipped inside it, next to a string of copied-down account numbers and email addresses, was a USB memory stick.

'Downloaded a batch of browser cookies and firewall settings, have you?' I asked, wiping snot off my upper lip with Liz's hanky.

'Never seen that before in my life,' snarled Auntie Sharon.

Miss Bennett handed her phone to Oliver, while trying to keep a grip of the wriggling woman beneath her. 'Here, call the police. Then call the school. We'll need to speak to all your parents.'

Once the police had taken charge of Auntie Sharon, and been given the address where they'd find 'Monsieur Jacques', we all returned to school in the minibus. Miss Bennett's entire class gave me a huge cheer, which was nice, and Harry Lovecraft got called to the Head's office, which was even nicer.

As it turned out, the police had been on the trail of Uncle 'Jacques' Lovecraft for half a dozen different crimes. Although, I'm sorry to say, impersonating a Frenchman wasn't one of them. Auntie Sharon's USB stick was shown to contain the personal details of seventy-seven local people, and of another two hundred and thirty from other parts of the country.

Unfortunately, that low-down rat Harry Lovecraft got off scott-free. His uncle and auntie denied his involvement, and he denied even knowing his uncle and auntie. In the end, there was no firm evidence against him – the money for those new goodies of his could have come from anywhere – and the Head had to drop the matter.

At the start of lessons the following day, he glided past me with a sneer so extreme it almost fell off his face.

'Don't think I'm going to forget this, Smart,' he whispered. 'One day, I'll have my revenge. One day.'

'Looking forward to it,' I said, with a polite smile.

That afternoon, I retreated to my shed, and my Thinking Chair. I propped my feet up on my desk, and jotted down some notes for my files.

Case closed.

Also available

SAXBY SMART
PRIVATE DETECTIVE

THE CURSE OF THE ANCIENT MASK
and other case files

My name is Saxby Smart and I'm a private detective. I go to St Egbert's School, my office is in the garden shed, and these are my case files.

In this book Saxby solves three of his most puzzling cases: The Curse of the Ancient Mask, The Mark of the Purple Homework and The Clasp of Doom. In each story Saxby gives you, the reader, clues which help solve the mystery. Are you 'smart' enough to find the answers?

Talk about being involved in a book! Sharp reads written in a lively and snappy style. Liverpool Echo

Coming soon

The
Pirate's Blood
and other case files

A ghostly handprint inside a museum case containing pirate treasure, a new classmate with a mysterious secret, and a strange case of arson in a bookshop . . .

In this third book, Saxby Smart – schoolboy detective – solves three more fascinating cases.

☆

www.piccadillypress.co.uk

☆ The latest news on forthcoming books

☆ Chapter previews

☆ Author biographies

☆ Fun quizzes

☆ Reader reviews

☆ Competitions and fab prizes

☆ Book features and cool downloads

☆ And much, much more . . .

Log on and check it out!

Piccadilly Press

☆